"Peagoose! But of course I love you! Why the devil else would I want you to be my life's companion!"

Her eyes widened in startled disbelief. He laughed and drew her into his arms. Slowly, lovingly his sensuous mouth descended on hers, and he kissed her with a fierce passion that demanded and received a like response from her. When at last he lifted his head, she stared at him wonderingly.

"I did not think that you wanted either me or my love."

"Not want you, you divine creature! I have been fascinated by you since that day we met in the park."

"So fascinated that you did not even ask my name!"

Fawcett Crest Books
by Marlene Suson:

THE DUKE'S REVENGE

AN INFAMOUS BARGAIN

THE RELUCTANT HEIRESS

THE DUKE'S REVENGE

Marlene Suson

FAWCETT CREST • NEW YORK

A Fawcett Crest Book
Published by Ballantine Books
Copyright © 1987 by Marlene Suson

Library of Congress Catalog Card Number: 87-90769

ISBN 0-449-21214-9

Manufactured in the United States of America

First Edition: July 1987

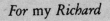
For my *Richard*

Chapter 1

An elegant curricle with a crest that proclaimed nobility stopped in front of one of the narrow, modest houses that lined a respectable but far from fashionable London street, causing a sensation among the neighbors. Even after the equipage's occupant, a young gentleman dressed in the first stare of fashion, disappeared into the house, curtains at several windows along the street continued to twitch. Bolder neighbors found reason for a sudden walk past the curricle drawn by two matched grays and guarded by a groom in resplendent livery. The street had never before enjoyed a visit from the aristocracy, and curiosity about the young man and his identity was intense.

Very little was known about the family that he was visiting, for it had moved into the neighborhood only a few days before. The household consisted of a mother and two daughters. The younger, a vulgar, voluptuous creature of eighteen with smoldering eyes and pouting lips, favored her mother. The elder, in her mid-twenties, was tall, with a lovely, delicate face and a regal carriage. She had about her an unconscious dignity that proclaimed quality. So different were the two daughters that several of the neighbors questioned whether they could truly be sisters.

In fact, they were half sisters. The elder, Alyssa Eliot,

was born of her twice-widowed mother's first marriage, while the younger, Rosina Raff, was a child of the second.

Ten minutes after the young gentleman left the house and drove off in his splendid curricle, the elder daughter, smartly dressed in a striped green bonnet, green spencer, and white kid gloves, was seen returning home.

As she entered the house, her mama's agitated voice screeched from the drawing room, "Come here at once, Alyssa. It is urgent."

Without taking the time to remove her bonnet or gloves, Alyssa hurried to her mother, who was reclining on a long mahogany settee, three chair backs wide, covered in a flowered needlepoint of many colors. It was part of a suite of two matching settees, twelve oversize armchairs, and four stools, all crammed into a small room that could have held only a third of the furniture comfortably.

"What's wrong, Mama?" Alyssa asked, her alarm reflected in her expressive face.

"You odious creature," Mrs. Fanny Raff replied petulantly, "why did you not warn me that the marquess of Stanwood would be calling today? I had no notion that you were even acquainted with him."

"The marquess came *here*!" Alyssa's appalled accents proclaimed that she was as shocked as her mama had been.

Mrs. Raff studied the only child of her first marriage critically for a long moment before saying, "I must declare, Alyssa, that I never thought you would make such a brilliant match. Nor, for that matter, any match at all! As long in the tooth as you are, I was quite certain that you were on the shelf."

Alyssa stared at Mrs. Raff as though she were speaking gibberish. "Mama, what are you talking about?"

"The marquess asked my permission for your hand in marriage."

The horrified look on Alyssa's face was not at all the reaction that one would have expected from a woman who

2

had just received a most illustrious and advantageous offer. "Surely, Mama, you did not grant it!"

Mrs. Raff regarded her dismayed daughter with sincere astonishment. "But of course I did! Why, he is one of the richest prizes on the marriage mart. And such a pleasing young man, too."

"He's not merely young," Alyssa cried. "He is *very* young! Scarcely nineteen, and I am twenty-five."

Mrs. Raff winced at Alyssa's blunt declaration of her age. It was just like the odious girl to remind her poor mama that she had a daughter of such advanced years.

"Furthermore," Alyssa was saying with considerable feeling, "you are quite mad to think that the haughty duke of Carlyle would allow his son and heir to marry a woman so far beneath his touch as I am. His Grace would never permit such a shocking mésalliance."

Even so bold a woman as Mrs. Raff shrank from the thought of incurring the wrath of the formidable duke, but she said defensively, "You, too, are of noble blood."

That was only half-true. There was nothing noble about Mrs. Raff's family, merchants all. But Alyssa's late father had been a descendant of one of Britain's most distinguished families, and her paternal grandfather was that noted historian and peer, Lord Eliot.

"Stanwood's blood is more than noble; it is royal," Alyssa retorted. "His papa is the king's cousin, and his mama was a granddaughter of King Louis the Fifteenth."

Mrs. Raff, dazzled by the prospect of having a daughter aligned with royalty, cried, "Oh-h-h, I shall be so proud."

Alyssa's speaking green eyes were sad. "Proud of a daughter who would be justly branded a brazen cradle robber?" she asked softly.

"The age difference is a trifle awkward," Mrs. Raff conceded.

"What the marquess feels for me is naught but calf love that he will quickly outgrow," Alyssa said firmly.

3

"Then you must leg-shackle him at once," her mama said, much alarmed that such a rich prize might slip away.

"Mama, I will not marry a codling too young to know his own mind," Alyssa said, once again displaying that lamentable stubbornness that she undoubtedly had inherited from her odious paternal grandfather.

Mrs. Raff wondered angrily why she had been cursed with a daughter so vexingly mutton-headed that she could consider rejecting a marquess's offer. Her darling Rosina, the daughter of her second marriage, would never be such a sapskull. Furthermore, any man who did not have windmills in his head would prefer her younger daughter's sensual face, voluptuous form, and glorious profusion of tumbling black curls that made Alyssa's neat auburn locks look quite insipid.

Rosina was a beauty, the image of her mother at the same age, while Alyssa was, in Mrs. Raff's critical opinion, too tall, too thin, and too proper. Men's interest was piqued by a little naughty promise in a woman. Worse, Alyssa's regal carriage accentuated her height, and she had an off-putting dignity about her. Instead of being flirtatious like Rosina, the impertinent chit had a disconcertingly blunt tongue and a lively sense of the ridiculous that Mrs. Raff, who had none at all, found deplorable.

Not even Alyssa's delicate face, which the most jaundiced observer would have to concede was lovely, pleased her mama, for the teasing green eyes, laughing mouth, and charming dimple in the cleft of her chin were all legacies from her father, who had been a severe disappointment to Mrs. Raff. She had maneuvered the son and heir of old Lord Eliot into the parson's mousetrap, thinking that she would enter the polite world and eventually become My Lady Eliot. Instead, His Lordship, as mean and cantankerous a man as ever lived, in Mrs. Raff's opinion, had disowned his son for his unpardonable folly in marrying the vulgar daughter of a Cit. Her husband's toplofty family and friends had had nothing more to do with him or his bride. When young Eliot died, he left his widow only debts and a daughter not yet out of leading strings.

Even now, more than a score of years later, Mrs. Raff was still bitter that she had been denied what she considered her rightful place in society by the vindictive Lord Eliot. But a son-in-law who was a marquess would surely secure for her and Rosina that much-coveted, long-denied position. Mrs. Raff was certain that the incomparable Rosina would immediately snare a duke. As for herself, she thought complacently, if inaccurately, that she was surely still beauty enough to capture a widowed lord as her third husband.

Alyssa, jerkily untying the strings of her striped bonnet with shaking fingers, said, "I will not marry the marquess."

"I declare you are the most vexing, pea-brained girl I have ever met," her mama snapped. "Only think you will be the duchess of Carlyle someday and so very rich."

"And so very unhappy wed to a man who will soon hate me for having taken advantage of his youth and inexperience."

Mrs. Raff shrugged complacently. "Once you have him riveted, you may go your separate ways. It is quite the acceptable thing among the aristocracy."

"It is not the acceptable thing with me," Alyssa retorted. "The thought of such a charade of a marriage chills me to the bone."

Mrs. Raff said scornfully, "So you want love. I declare that for a girl who was supposedly so well educated, you entertain some peculiarly silly notions. I cannot believe that you mean to reject Stanwood's suit."

"I mean to do exactly that!" Alyssa said resolutely, turning to leave the room.

Mrs. Raff, her dreams of a widowed lord for herself and a duke for Rosina crumbling, lashed out petulantly, "Oh, was there ever a more unnatural, unfeeling, ungrateful child! And after all I have done for you."

Anger flashed in Alyssa's green eyes as she paused in the doorway. "All you have done for me! Oh, Mama, that is doing it up too brown. What you did was abandon me upon my grandfather Eliot's doorstep when I was still in leading strings."

Although that was precisely what Mrs. Raff had done, she had long since managed to rationalize this action as a great sacrifice to assure her daughter's future, forgetting that it had been only her own future that had concerned her. After Jack Eliot's death, she had tried to get his father to take her in by mendaciously writing him that she and his granddaughter were in imminent danger of starving if he did not. He had replied that he would be overjoyed to see her suffer such a fate. However, if she would relinquish claim to his granddaughter, he would reluctantly agree to adopt and raise Alyssa. Her mother, who clearly saw that a squalling little brat would be a serious handicap to merry widowhood, was delighted to be relieved of her.

Upstairs, in the bedchamber that Alyssa shared with her half sister, she paced the floor in great agitation, horrified that the young marquess had so misread her friendly teasing manner as to think that she had a tendre for him and disgusted that her mama would approve such a singularly unsuitable match.

Alyssa knew that her mother had not loved either of her husbands. Her only consideration in marrying them had been for what they could provide her. She had badly misjudged what she would gain by marrying Jack Eliot, who had been no older than Stanwood when she had riveted him. But Mrs. Raff's second marriage had been more fruitful. Although the late Elias Raff had been a Cit who lacked the title and social position that his bride so coveted, he had been wealthy and had indulged her every selfish and extravagant whim.

But Alyssa was as different from her mother as the sun from the moon. If ever Alyssa married, it would be for love, even though she was not likely to find it at her advanced age. And she did not love the marquess. They had met a month ago at the house of Charlotte and Oliver Hagar, the only friends from Alyssa's former life who knew that she was in London.

Charlotte had been Alyssa's best friend since the two had attended the same select seminary for the daughters of Britain's most elite families. Even Charlotte's marriage two years earlier to Oliver Hagar, an aide to the first minister, had not weakened the friendship.

The Hagars were a lively couple, and their unceremonious household had been a haven for Alyssa since she had left Ormandy Park, her grandfather Eliot's country estate in Northumberland, to come to London to live with Mrs. Raff six weeks earlier. How Alyssa rued having agreed to do so, for those weeks beneath her mother's roof had been the most miserable of her life. She did not know what she would have done without the Hagars, who had been kindness itself to her. Oliver, knowing how she loved to ride, had even insisted that she use one of his hacks. So she rose early each morning, while fashionable London was still abed, to ride in the park when no one she might know would be about. It was always the high point of her day.

The marquess of Stanwood had been introduced to the Hagars' house by his uncle, Lord Sidney Carstair, a friend of Oliver's. Stanwood, in his first season on the town, had been excessively lonely and blue-deviled since his father had returned to Beauchamp, his country estate in Berkshire, leaving his son alone in London. The stripling's concerned uncle had brought him to the Hagars', thinking that the amusing company there would surely cheer the boy.

Feeling sorry for the young marquess, Alyssa had set about rescuing him from his fit of the dismals. He had confided to her that he had never been to London before and that he was not finding it to his liking. When she expressed astonishment that the heir of the worldly duke of Carlyle had not been to the capital, the marquess confessed that he and his younger sister, Ellen, had passed their entire lives at Beauchamp because their papa did not think the city healthy for children.

"He was reluctant for me to come to London even now, although it was he who said that I needed town bronze," the youth confessed. "He predicted that I would prefer the country, and as usual, he was right. I did not mind the city so much before he left London, for he took me everywhere, and he is lively company."

By all accounts, His Grace was indeed that. In his seventeen years as a widower—and, rumor had it, well before that—he had sampled a wide and varied array of female delights. In light of his notorious reputation, even Alyssa's blunt tongue lacked the courage to inquire what "everywhere" encompassed. Yet the marquess was so naive and innocent that she quickly surmised the duke must have given his son an expurgated introduction to London.

"Why has your papa abandoned you?" Alyssa asked, certain that he had gone off for a few days with one of his ladybirds.

"My little sister took ill, and Papa went back to Beauchamp to be with her. I miss him so!"

Alyssa, uncertain which caused her greater astonishment, given the duke's reputation, his concern for his daughter or his son's obvious love for him, stammered, "Is your sister's illness serious?"

"I don't think so, but Papa worries so about her. You see, she has been an invalid and very frail since she was born."

From that evening on, Alyssa had frequently enjoyed the young marquess's company at the Hagars'. He was possessed of such amiable disposition, generous nature, quick humor, naive candor, and impetuous enthusiasms that it was impossible not to like him. It quite amazed Alyssa that the duke of Carlyle—whose reputation was that of a harsh, haughty aristocrat who did not scruple to freeze a man with his consequence or destroy him with his power—could have produced such an unassuming, sweet-natured son. The only flaw that she had detected in the boy was a streak of passionate obstinacy, most likely a legacy from his father.

A knock at the bedroom door and the maid's voice calling, "Miss Raff," intruded on Alyssa's rumination, and she answered absently, "She isn't here," before she remembered that she was now Miss Raff. Her own surname had been forbidden to her as long as she lived with her mother, and in the six weeks that she had been with her parent, Alyssa had not yet fully adjusted to being called by her late stepfather's name.

"But, ma'am," the maid protested, "me knows your voice."

"I'm sorry," Alyssa apologized. "I thought you wanted Rosina."

"There's a young swell, the same one that was to see your mama earlier, awanting you in the drawing room. He calls himself a marquess," the girl said in an voice of awe tempered with skepticism. Lords did not come calling at such modest houses as this.

"Is Mama here?" Alyssa asked anxiously, not wanting to see her suitor in her mother's presence.

"No, she's been agone ten minutes or more now."

Alyssa gave fervent, silent thanks.

When she entered the small, overcrowded drawing room a few minutes later, the marquess greeted her with a shy smile on his lips and adoration in his brown eyes. Unlike so many young men of the day, he had not adopted the extravagant dress of a pink of the ton or even of a dandy. Although subdued, his clothes displayed an elegant taste that was unusual in one so young. His face was pleasant, although it was too round, and his lower lip too protruding

9

for him to be truly handsome, but one ceased to notice after a few minutes in his sunny company.

"Did your mama tell you?" he asked, a blush tinging his young face.

Alyssa smiled reassuringly. Although she had no intention of marrying the marquess, he was such a dear youth that she could not bear to hurt him. She knew how easily and severely the heart and pride of an ardent boy in the throes of first love could be wounded. Alyssa, feeling like a protective older sister toward an innocent little brother, was determined, if at all possible, to spare him any pain.

Furthermore, a stripling of his age doted on a challenge. A flat rejection of his suit, especially given the marquess's stubborn streak, would most likely only make him more determined to win her. She would have to employ another, more subtle way to discourage his tendre for her.

She began gently, "I was quite taken by surprise. It has been less than a month since we met at the Hagars' and—"

"Twenty-seven days, eighteen hours, and I think"—he paused to consult his fob watch—"thirty-four minutes. I knew before that evening had ended that you were the only woman for me," he concluded passionately.

"But you scarcely know me."

"I know you well enough to love you as I have never loved another woman," he declared still more passionately.

"You have only lately come up from the country," Alyssa said tactfully. "Perhaps a wider acquaintance among what London offers would be in order before you make your choice of a wife."

He stiffened indignantly. "You have no notion of all the females who have thrown themselves at me since I have been in London!"

In fact, Alyssa had a very good notion. Given Stanwood's title, lineage, and the great fortune he would one day inherit, every nubile young lady of quality and ambitious mama in London had undoubtedly tried to shackle him.

"And every one of them was so silly and insipid and dissembling," Stanwood continued in exasperation. "They told me only what they thought would please me. You are the one woman I have met in London who says what she truly thinks. And you are capital fun besides."

"But you met my family today." The stricken look on the marquess's young face told Alyssa how much that introduction had shocked him. "I cannot imagine that yours would welcome such a connection."

"You are so very different from them. I do not understand how you could have been raised under the same roof as . . ." His tongue seemed to tie itself in embarrassed knots.

Alyssa had not been, but she did not enlighten him to her true background. It would not help to discourage his suit if he learned that her surname was Eliot, not Raff, and that she came from a distinguished family on her father's side. She said gently, "You see, Jeremy, even you recognize what a mésalliance a match with me would be."

He stiffened indignantly. "You are trying to fob me off. But I shall have you! I adore you!" The marquess's amiable face hardened into mulish obstinacy. "If you will not have me now, I shall devote myself to winning you!"

With a sinking heart, Alyssa perceived that she was doing exactly what she did not want to do: making the winning of her hand a challenge to him, so that he was fired with stubborn determination to have her. His interest was far more likely to wane if he thought her already his, especially if she then conducted herself so that he would soon rue having won her.

"I will not accept no for an answer!" he cried in a recalcitrant, impassioned voice.

She said soothingly, "Then I shall not say no, but only on one condition."

Although she had been careful not to say yes, either, he misinterpreted her answer as acquiescence. "I shall make you so happy."

Alyssa did not correct his mistaken impression that she had accepted his offer. Instead, she said, "You did not agree to my condition."

"What is it?"

"That we keep our *romance* secret," she said, deliberately avoiding the word betrothal.

The happiness on Jeremy's face gave way to dismay. "For how long?"

"A year." That would give her plenty of time to cure his tendre for her. In truth, she was certain that it would not take her more than a few weeks.

The marquess was crestfallen. "A year! Why? I planned that we should be wed by then."

"No! I could not bear to have it said that I am a wicked hussy who snatched her husband from his cradle before he was old enough to know his own mind!" she cried dramatically. "Oh, I should die of shame! If you love me, you will not subject me to such humiliation!"

"No, no, of course not," her young suitor stammered.

"Besides, I cannot conceive that your papa would permit you to wed so young."

"He was married and had two children by my age. He will not—he cannot—stop me!"

"Yes, he can. You must have his permission until you reach your majority, and that is two years away," she reminded him.

Jeremy said mutinously, "If he refuses his permission, we shall elope to Gretna Green."

Alyssa managed a horrified shriek. "We shall do no such thing! Think of the scandal! Think of my reputation. How can you ask such a thing of me?"

Stanwood was instantly contrite, and she pushed home her advantage. "You must swear that you will tell no one of our secret." Again she deliberately avoided using the word betrothal.

"No one. Except Papa."

That was the last person Alyssa wanted to think that she was betrothed to his son. From all that she had heard about the duke, he was a merciless opponent. The thought of what he would do if he thought her engaged to his son made her cry in alarm, "No, you most particularly must not tell your papa! Promise me that you shall not!"

"I must tell him," Jeremy said stubbornly. "I have never kept a secret from him in my life."

"Then I reject your offer!" She held up her hand to silence his protest. "No, I am adamant. Do not waste your breath!"

"Why, I believe you are afraid of him," the marquess said wonderingly, "but you should not be. He is the very best of fathers."

Which, if true, was precisely why she should be terrified of him, Alyssa thought grimly. He would be justly outraged by such a mésalliance for his son.

"All right," Jeremy said reluctantly. "I promise not to tell Papa, but I cannot like keeping it from him. I know that once you meet, you and Papa will get along famously."

More likely infamously! Alyssa thought, praying that Jeremy's puppy love would end quickly. If the duke learned that his son considered himself betrothed to her, Carlyle's fury would surely be monumental.

Chapter 2

If anything, Alyssa underestimated His Grace the Duke of Carlyle's rage upon learning about her.

The young marquess, true to the letter if not the spirit of his word to Alyssa, did not tell his father. Nevertheless, word reached the duke at Beauchamp that very day.

After leaving Alyssa, the marquess, wishing to buy his betrothed a gift befitting a future duchess, went to see Mr. Hugh Page. This gentleman held a unique position with the duke, whom he had served for seventeen years with intelligence, devotion, and dedication. As Carlyle's trusted majordomo and confidant in all matters of business, no man alive knew more about His Grace's affairs, both financial and personal, than Hugh Page.

The duke kept his son on a tight financial leash, and the jewels that Stanwood wanted to purchase would necessitate his receiving several months of his allowance in advance from Mr. Page, a request that not unnaturally aroused that astute gentleman's curiosity. Somehow, under his adroit questioning, Stanwood let slip his happy news.

To His Lordship's dismay, instead of felicitating him, Mr. Page said sharply, "You must tell your father."

"But I cannot!"

"Why do you not wish him to know?"

Since Stanwood wanted nothing more than to tell his

father, who had always been more like an indulgent older brother than a stern papa to him, he said frankly, "I *do* want him to know, but Alyssa insists on keeping it a secret. She made me promise particularly that I would not tell Papa. I think that she is afraid of him."

And well she should be, Mr. Page thought. The sketchy details that he had subtly extracted from Stanwood had given him an unpleasant picture of the youth's intended. Mr. Page was not a betting man, but he would be willing to wager a year's salary that Alyssa Raff would soon be very sorry indeed that she had set her cap for the duke's son.

"If you cannot tell your father, then I shall," Mr. Page said. "That way *you* will not have told him and, therefore, *you* will not have broken your promise to your betrothed."

Mr. Page's solution greatly appealed to Jeremy. However, out of deference to his betrothed's wishes, he demurred. "No, I cannot permit you to tell Papa."

"You cannot stop me. If Miss Raff complains, you may heap all the blame upon me for treacherously betraying both your confidence and your wishes."

This mollified Jeremy's opposition, but he said uneasily, "Neither you nor Papa can tell anyone else. Alyssa insists that our betrothal must remain a secret."

"Rest assured that our lips will be sealed," Mr. Page said with an irony that was lost on the marquess.

After Stanwood's departure, Hugh Page set about discovering all that he could about one Alyssa Raff. What little information he gleaned so appalled him that instead of carrying the news to Beauchamp the following morning as he had intended, he went late that afternoon on the fastest horse that Marsh's excellent stables could provide him.

With each passing mile, his dread of the forthcoming session with Carlyle increased. For all the duke's reputation as a rake, he was as loving and devoted a father as Hugh had ever seen and would take the news of his son's folly badly. Hugh hated being the bearer of such unhappy tidings to a man whom he held in affection and esteem. Despite Carlyle's ruthless reputation, he was always kind and generous to the few people he truly cared about, and he had demonstrated toward Hugh a courtesy and a confidence that was unheard of in employers. During their many years together, Mr. Page had come to understand the duke very well indeed and, as a result, would have walked through fire for His Grace.

By the time Hugh Page was escorted into the presence of Richard Jeremy William Carstair, the eighth duke of Carlyle, in the great library at Beauchamp, he was roundly cursing Stanwood for having made him the recipient of his blasted secret.

"To what do I owe the pleasure of this rare visit to Beauchamp, Hugh?" the duke asked with an engaging smile as Mr. Page made his bow.

"Your Grace will find it no pleasure," Hugh said grimly.

Carlyle raised one of his thick, dark eyebrows questioningly. It was easy for Hugh to see why the duke cut such a notorious swath among the ladies, both highborn and high-flying. He was a dashingly handsome figure. With a lean, trim body that needed no corset, brown hair as thick as it was curly, and a lithe grace, he looked younger than his thirty-six years. His voice was deep, pleasant, and deceptively soft. A pair of glittering, penetrating eyes, hazel flecked with gold, beneath heavy brows dominated his aristocratically sculpted face with its perfectly proportioned nose and sensual mouth. The hardness of these remarkable eyes, the unusual thickness of his dark brows that could knit together in a fierce scowl, coupled with his utter disregard for others' opinions of his behavior, had contributed quite as much as that behavior itself to his fearsome reputation.

Hugh, however, knew a different man, especially when he was surrounded by his family at Beauchamp. How much more relaxed and easygoing His Grace was there than in London, where he habitually wore a harshly cynical countenance.

And there was nothing that he was more cynical about than women. And why not? Hugh thought, the way so many of them shamelessly threw themselves at him. Carlyle was generally pursued rather than pursuer, but he was a quarry willing to be caught. Yet he made no false promises. He was forthright about matrimony being a trap in which no woman would ever again catch him. Having long ago fulfilled his obligation to produce an heir, he wanted nothing more to do with marriage. Not that he trifled with innocents. Knowing the rules of the game he played so well, he confined his amours to sophisticated beauties of the ton and to the fashionable impures. His liaisons were always brief, by his choice, not the lady's.

"Such a face, Hugh, alarms me," Carlyle observed. "What is it?"

Reluctantly, Hugh broke the news of the marquess's betrothal. For the first time in all the years that Hugh had known him, the duke was robbed of speech.

"I tried to point out his youth to him," Hugh said to fill the silence, "but he only reminded me that you were married when you were sixteen."

"Yes! Thrust into a marriage bed when I was hardly more than a child myself, with a woman six years my senior. A woman I hardly knew." The duke's words were permeated with such bitterness that Hugh flinched. "I should never have left Jeremy in London when Ellen fell ill and I had to return here."

"How is Lady Ellen now?" Hugh asked.

"Recovered." Relief softened the duke's face so that he looked almost boyish. "My sister Hester is taking her to Bath in the morning to partake of the waters for a month." His handsome face hardened again. "Who is this chit who has so enchanted my son? Some silly young flirt scarcely out of the schoolroom, with coaxing ways?''

"Hardly. She is five-and-twenty.''

"*Five-and-twenty!* Jeremy's scarcely nineteen.'' His thick brows snapped together in the Carlyle scowl. "If she has been on the town all these years, I must know her.''

"Her name is Alyssa Raff.''

"I never heard of her.''

"I am relieved.''

The duke's hard eyes narrowed. "Explain.''

"She is the elder of two daughters. Her mother is the widow of a Cit who died last year, leaving her in much reduced circumstances. In the past two months, her fortunes have mysteriously improved.'' A deep frown creased Hugh's face. "I have not yet seen Alyssa, but I was able to observe her mother and younger sister as they returned home this afternoon.''

"That bad?'' asked the duke, correctly interpreting Hugh's expression. "What does the sister look like?''

Hugh grimaced. "Very much like that dreadful barque of frailty from whose clutches you had to extract Lord Sidney when he first went on the town.''

"Good God!'' the duke exclaimed.

"Mrs. Raff and her younger daughter are clearly ill-bred, tasteless, vulgar females. Frankly, Your Grace, I was shocked.''

"Then why on earth would you think that I might know of Alyssa Raff?''

Hugh colored slightly. "I fear it would not have been in honorable circumstances. From what little I was able to learn, I fear there is something very havey-cavey about her. Mrs. Raff recently moved from the large house where she had lived for nine years into more modest quarters, and I interviewed several of her former neighbors. In all the years that she resided in the large house, Alyssa did not live with her, although she occasionally made brief visits, arriving in an elegant carriage accompanied by servants in expensive livery. It is only during the past few weeks that she has again been under her mother's roof. Her return to the family home, by the way, coincided with the improvement in her mother's fortunes.''

Carlyle's face was as black as the sky during a thunderstorm. He was notorious for his blunt speech, and he did not mince words now. ''Under whose protection was the strumpet living?''

''I was not able to ascertain that,'' Hugh answered, relieved that His Grace had immediately drawn the same conclusion about Miss Raff that he had.

Within twenty minutes, the duke's household was in an uproar, following his announcement that he was leaving immediately by horseback for London, not waiting even for his valet, Thompson, who was to follow the next morning after packing what wardrobe his master would require in London. Although the scandalized Thompson could not imagine that His Grace could survive a night in London without his assistance, one look at Carlyle's furious face silenced the protest his loyal valet had been about to voice. Never, he confided later to the butler, had he seen His Grace in such a pelter.

As his horse galloped through the night toward London, the duke of Carlyle seethed at the aging, scheming doxy who had ensnared his son.

How cleverly Miss Raff must have woven her net around Jeremy, taking advantage of his youth and inexperience. The duke was particularly incensed by her extracting a promise from the boy that he would not tell his father of his betrothal. Of course she did not want him to learn of it, for the cunning jade knew full well that he would nip her little romance in the bud. She knew, too, that Jeremy could not marry for two years without his father's permission. Her plan must be to lure the boy into an elopement to Gretna Green before his family became aware of his involvement with her. Well, she would not succeed!

Carlyle knew from his own bitter marriage the misery and disillusionment in store for a green youth who fell in love with a sophisticated, faithless woman several years older than himself. He clenched his hand around his mount's reins. He was determined to save Jeremy, whom he dearly loved, from such suffering.

His Grace had known that London would be a dangerous place for a youth as amiable and naive as his son and had postponed his introduction to it for as long as he could. With Jeremy's great expectations, he was certain to be pursued on the one hand by an army of marriageable young ladies and determined mamas eager to lure the future duke of Carlyle into marriage, and on the other hand by male parasites equally eager to lead him into the dissolute life that claimed so many young sons of rich fathers. When Carlyle had reluctantly brought his son at last to London, it was with a determination to make him aware of both dangers.

The second had been the easier to deal with. The boy, who loved the country and its pleasures, liked London even less than Carlyle had expected he would. To his father's relief, Jeremy had no taste for gambling and whoring and hell-raising. He had quickly grasped how silly and empty and ultimately unsatisfying was the life led by so many young men in London.

He was less discerning, however, about the motives and true nature of the resolute young ladies and their mamas who sought to shackle him. So with patience and humor, Carlyle subtly pointed out their wiles and ruses, seizing every opportunity to mock their machinations, flirtatious coyness, and insincere tongues.

It was not that he objected to his son's marrying, but he wanted for him a wife who would love him for himself, not for the title and fortune he would inherit, an intelligent, good-humored woman with a domestic nature, who would be content with the country life that Jeremy preferred and would devote herself to her husband and children instead of yearning for London's frivolous society, entertainments, and flirtations.

His Grace was determined to spare Jeremy the heartbreak and disillusionment that he himself had suffered. Which was why the duke would never permit Miss Raff to become his daughter-in-law. He cursed himself for having left Jeremy alone in London with no one but Sidney to look out for him. Carlyle had thought it safe to do so because he had been certain that Jeremy had absorbed his father's subtle lessons about the deceits and trickery of determined females. But clearly the duke had been wrong, or his son would not have been encoiled by a cunning hussy.

The night had been clear when Carlyle had left Beauchamp, but now, as he neared London, clouds that promised rain moved across the sky, hiding the moon and stars. He urged his mount on, hoping to reach Grosvenor Square before he was drenched.

If only Jeremy had come to him about Miss Raff. His Grace's anger at the betrothal paled beside the hurt he felt over Jeremy's failure to tell him about the wretched doxy. Until now he had enjoyed an extraordinarily close relationship with his son. Never before had Jeremy kept a secret from his sire, and the duke attributed this uncharacteristic behavior to the power that evil Jezebel had over his besotted young son. One thing was certain: Before he was done with Miss Alyssa Raff, she would regret the day that she had met his son.

Chapter 3

One of Alyssa's economies was mending torn garments instead of discarding them. When her mother returned home that evening, she was in the drawing room repairing a petticoat of Rosina's. Hearing Mrs. Raff's shrill voice in the hall, Alyssa lifted her head from her sewing and looked about the room. Her mother had insisted upon jamming every piece of elaborate, oversize furniture from the much larger drawing room of her previous home into it, giving it all the homey charm of a storage shed.

In the hall the maid-of-all-work told Mrs. Raff about the marquess's second visit. She rushed to her elder daughter, demanding to know whether she had rejected Stanwood's suit.

"No, but—"

"I declare you have at last developed a little sense!" her mother exclaimed.

Alyssa, who had no intention of revealing her strategy for handling Jeremy to her mother, hastily changed the subject. "Do you and Rosina go to Vauxhall tonight?" The pleasure garden was one of Mama's favorite places, and she went there frequently with her younger daughter.

"Yes." Noticing for the first time what Alyssa was doing, Mrs. Raff demanded irritably, "Why do you bother with that? Rosina wishes a new one."

"We cannot afford a new one," Alyssa said calmly, continuing to ply her needle.

"It is not fitting for a future marchioness to be mending petticoats," Mrs. Raff complained. "When will the marquess tell his father about your betrothal?"

"He won't. I made him promise that he would not."

Mrs. Raff stared at Alyssa as though she had taken leave of her senses. "In heaven's name, why?"

Alyssa sighed. Her mother was a foolish woman, but surely even she must realize that only grief would come to them if Carlyle learned of his son's offer. Alyssa tried to explain this, but her mother brushed aside her concern, saying smugly, "The duke will drop his opposition when he sees what a scandal I will create if his son tries to renege on his promise."

"Oh, Mama," Alyssa said pityingly as she thought of Carlyle's notorious reputation, "the duke does not care a whit what the world thinks of him, and I warn you that he would be a lethal adversary."

"If you are so afraid of him, I am surprised that you accepted his son's offer."

"I did not accept it."

Mrs. Raff's face was bewildered. "But you said—"

"I said I did not reject it. Although he considers us betrothed, I have no intention of marrying him."

"You provoking chit!" Mrs. Raff cried angrily, stalking from the room. At the door, she paused to screech, "I wish, Alyssa, that you would go back to your grandfather!"

If only she could! But Alyssa knew that it would be months before Lord Eliot's temper cooled sufficiently to permit her to return to him. How Alyssa regretted her decision to disobey him and come to her mother.

After Mr. Raff had been so disobliging as to die last year with an estate shockingly depleted by his wife's years of extravagance, she and Rosina, unaccustomed to economy, soon became mired in debt. Mrs. Raff wrote her elder daughter, who was living with her grandfather at Ormandy Park, his country house in Northumberland, begging her to save her mother, who was about to be thrown into debtors' prison.

"My finances and my fate are in your hands," Mrs. Raff had written. "I beg of you not to desert your poor, loving mama in her time of dire need."

Although the poor, loving mama had been happy to relinquish Alyssa to be raised by her paternal grandfather, she had not severed all association with her. Realizing that a well-connected daughter could be useful someday, she had insisted that her "beloved" child be permitted to visit her for two weeks each year. To her amazement, Lord Eliot had readily agreed. Alyssa understood very well, although Mrs. Raff did not, why he had done so. Those visits, which Alyssa had dreaded and loathed, revealed to her with far more clarity than anything else could have her mama's vulgar, selfish, scheming nature.

Yet Mrs. Raff was her mother, and her frantic pleas for help sorely troubled Alyssa. She could not permit her own mother to rot in debtors' prison. But Alyssa had no money of her own and was entirely dependent upon her grandfather. He, of course, would never give Mrs. Raff a shilling. So the only help Alyssa, who was a notable manager, could offer was to go to London to try to straighten out her extravagant parent's finances. Alyssa had not wanted to leave Ormandy Park, but she had felt it her filial duty to do so, a view not shared by her grandfather. He had pointed out that her loving mama had had no compunction about abandoning Alyssa on his doorstep.

When Alyssa had persisted in her determination to go to her mother, Lord Eliot, a domestic tyrant of the first water, had flown into a towering rage, swearing that he would have nothing more to do with her if she went to that scheming, vulgar hussy who had robbed him of his favorite son, then dispatched the poor boy to an early grave. Not only would he not allow Alyssa to return to Ormandy Park, he would not permit her to disgrace his name by using it while residing in that hussy's house. Alyssa must assume her late stepfather's name and never mention her connection with the Eliots.

Her grandfather had been so apoplectic that she had finally agreed to this unreasonable demand, fearing that if she did not, he would suffer a stroke.

Although she thought his demand silly, she was a woman of her word. Since coming to London, she had scrupulously adhered to her promise, carefully avoiding everyone who might know her true identity, except the Hagars, who obligingly kept it secret, introducing her as Alyssa Raff.

The duke of Carlyle arrived at his mansion in Grosvenor Square that night just as Jeremy was leaving.

"Papa, you are back!" Jeremy cried, his face lighting up with unmistakable delight at the sight of his father in the elegant entry with its shimmering crystal chandelier, beechwood chairs, and marble floor. "I have missed you so."

"Have you?" The duke smiled affectionately at his son, who bore little resemblance to his father except for his dark, curly hair and elegant, upcut nose. Jeremy had the round face and protruding lower lip of Carlyle's late duchess, but his amiable nature, so unlike hers, and his passionate enthusiasms reminded the duke of the sunny, innocent boy that he himself had been at sixteen.

Noticing his father's travel-stained riding coat, breeches, and boots, Jeremy frowned. "Surely, Papa, you did not ride up from Beauchamp on horseback?"

"It was a nice night for a ride," Carlyle said dryly. "Where are you bound now?"

"To show George Braden the town. He arrived only

today from Northumberland and has never been to London before. Would you like to join us?''

''No,'' the duke said, losing interest in the expedition when it did not include Miss Raff. ''I have someone I must see tonight at Vauxhall. What have you been doing in London during my absence, Jeremy? Anything of import that I should know of?''

The marquess blushed guiltily. His gaze dropped to the polished marble floor, and he did not see the angry tightening of his father's lips. The duke's tone, however, remained light. ''What is it, Jeremy? Do you have something to tell me?''

The youth fidgeted with the buttons on his waistcoat and looked miserably unhappy. ''No, sir.''

Stung by his son's failure to confide in him, the duke silently cursed Miss Alyssa Raff. Lifting a questioning eyebrow, he asked, ''Nothing at all?''

Instead of answering, Jeremy burst out, ''When will you be seeing Mr. Page?''

''I have seen him, and I am disappointed, Jeremy.'' Carlyle's voice was gently reproachful. ''I had thought that when you decided to wed, I would be the very first to hear of it, and from your own lips.''

The youth's gaze flew up to the duke's eyes. ''You know! I am so glad!''

The relief that shone on Jeremy's face was echoed in his father's heart as he realized that his son had not wished to keep the betrothal secret from him.

''I wanted more than anything to tell you, but Alyssa made me swear that I would not.''

''How very odd that she would want you to keep your happy news a secret from your own father.''

''I think she fears that you will prohibit me from marrying her.'' Jeremy looked suddenly worried. ''You won't, will you?''

Carlyle longed to issue just such a prohibition, but he

knew the boy's obstinate streak too well to do anything so foolish as that. Instead, he would have to handle Jeremy with the greatest of tact. Concealing his seething anger at the vulgar hussy who had entrapped his son, he said, "Of course not."

Relief shone on Jeremy's face. "I knew that you would not, but she did not believe me."

Although her skepticism was well founded, Carlyle asked innocently, "Why not? Does she think herself beneath your touch?"

"Oh, no, not at all!" his son replied with greater haste than accuracy.

"I thought not," his father said with heavy irony. "Tell me about her."

"I cannot find words," began Jeremy, who then proceeded to find a great many of them, mostly effusive adjectives, to describe his intended. He painted her as such a paragon of beauty, virtue, intelligence, and wit that his father raged silently at how completely Jeremy, normally an intelligent boy, had been blinded by the trollop. Carlyle knew how vulnerable and sensitive a young cub in the throes of first love was, and his heart ached for the heartbreak and humiliation that Jeremy would inevitably suffer at Miss Raff's callous hands. "How old is the divine Alyssa?"

Jeremy ran a finger between his neck and his cravat as though that garment had suddenly grown exceedingly tight. "A trifling older than I."

"What is a trifling—a week or two?"

Jeremy's face reddened. "She is five-and-twenty."

"What an odd definition you have of a trifling," the duke observed wryly, wondering again under whose protection the doxy had been living the past nine years. "How is it, if she has been on the town all these years, I have never met her?"

"She dislikes society and avoids it."

The duke's eyes narrowed. No doubt she did so because she feared recognition by someone who knew her sordid past and would reveal it to his son. "When shall I meet her?"

Jeremy said evasively, "Perhaps in a few days."

"Why not now? I confess to a great curiosity about any woman possessed of so many charms as the divine Alyssa, especially when she will be the future duchess of Carlyle."

"I dare not introduce you because she said that she would end our betrothal if I told you of it. While it was not *I* who did so, I fear that she will be very angry when she learns you know." Jeremy's face suddenly brightened. "But surely she will forgive me when I tell her that we have your permission to marry immediately."

Reluctant as he was to tell his stubborn son so, the duke said quietly, "But you do not have that permission yet."

"Why not?" the boy demanded indignantly. "Surely you cannot wish me to marry one of those odious young ladies at Almack's who have been casting lures for me. You yourself pointed out what silly creatures they are."

At least his son had learned to appraise correctly the overeager young ladies of Almack's. Too bad, Carlyle thought wearily, that he had not also schooled Jeremy about cyprians. Forcing a smile to his lips, the duke said, "Gudgeon! I do not at all wish you to rivet yourself to one of them. Such a foolish, insipid creature would never make you happy. And, believe me, all I want for you is happiness."

"If that is the case," Jeremy cried passionately, "you will give me your permission to marry Alyssa!"

"Before I have met her?" the duke asked gently, deciding to use Miss Raff's insistence that he not be told of the betrothal to his advantage. It gave him a way to buy time, and given enough time, he would see that Jeremy came to recognize the Jezebel for what she was. "Surely, you cannot expect me to give my permission until after I have met her?''

The love-struck youth reluctantly agreed. ''No, Papa.''

His Grace observed gently, ''I would think a woman of five-and-twenty would find a youth barely nineteen too young for her.''

''Don't tell me that I am too young to wed,'' Jeremy cried, firing up. ''You were married by my age!''

''I was a widower with two children to raise by your age, and it is not an experience that I wish for you.'' A wave of profound bitterness swept over Carlyle at the memory of himself as a bridegroom, so young, so in love, and the humiliation and heartbreak that followed.

''I will marry Alyssa!'' Jeremy cried rebelliously. ''You cannot stop me from doing so.''

''I did not say that I would, so pray do not fly into the boughs without reason,'' his father said calmly. ''I would, however, prefer that you wait a few months.''

''Why?'' Jeremy demanded mulishly.

''Most importantly, for your bride's reputation. Such a hurried march to the altar as you propose with a woman so many years your senior will convince the world that you compromised her and were forced to wed. I am persuaded that if you love her, you would not wish to cast such a black shadow upon her virtue.''

''No, of course not!'' Jeremy exclaimed, instantly contrite. ''Oh, Papa, once you meet Alyssa, you will find it impossible not to love her as much as I do.''

More likely, thought His Grace, he would find it impossible not to throttle the strumpet.

Chapter 4

When Mrs. Raff and Rosina came down the staircase that night, bound for Vauxhall Gardens, Alyssa stared at them in speechless dismay, giving silent thanks that she was not accompanying them.

Although simple muslin gowns like those that Alyssa wore were now the style among the ton, her mother's notion of fashion was based on what had been the mode twenty-five years ago. Mrs. Raff firmly believed that ladies of quality wore only the most elaborate of satin and silk gowns. Although fate and that spiteful old Lord Eliot had denied her her rightful place in that company, she was determined to dress the part.

She had outdone herself tonight, choosing a polonaise gown in brilliant red satin. Its three enormous panniers had been drawn up by gold cords that ended in long tassels and exaggerated her ample proportions. Despite the evidence in her mirror to the contrary, Mrs. Raff was blind to the substantial increase over the years in her girth. But no one else who saw her tonight would be.

Her elaborate, heavily powdered coiffure, which was as out of fashion as her gown, depended upon several hairpieces for its height. Her face was painted a sickly white, enlivened by two brilliant patches of color on the cheeks and a large black patch near her mouth.

The late Mr. Raff, constantly harassed by his wife's demands for jewelry, had discovered that she lacked an eye that could discern real gems from paste, and thereafter he had frequently gifted her with baubles as gaudy as they were fraudulent. Tonight she had contrived to load her person with an astonishing number of them.

Rosina's purple satin gown clashed violently with the red that her mother wore, and its circassienne style, too, was outmoded. Her waist was laced so tightly that she could not take a deep breath, and the bodice was cut so shockingly low that Alyssa blushed.

When at last Alyssa recovered her voice, she said faintly, "Your dress is very bright, Mama."

"I have always preferred vivid colors," Mrs. Raff replied proudly. "They capture a man's eye."

"But is it not too elaborate for Vauxhall?" Alyssa asked, tactfully trying to prevent her mama from making a cake of herself.

"The mother-in-law of the future duke of Carlyle must look the part," Mrs. Raff said grandly.

Alyssa refrained from pointing out that her mother was not now, and never would be, that.

Mrs. Raff continued, "It shall not be said that I look dowdy."

"No, Mama," Alyssa said, knowing with embarrassed certainty what it would be said that she did look like.

After Mrs. Raff and Rosina departed, Alyssa went slowly up the narrow staircase to her bedchamber, threw herself down on her bed, and wondered morosely what would happen to her if her grandfather did not relent and permit her return to Ormandy Park. Since coming to London to help her mother had cost her, perhaps permanently, the only real home she had ever known, Alyssa had been more than a little angry to discover that, as usual, her mother had exaggerated her situation in the hope that her daughter would wheedle a handsome sum from Lord Eliot so that Mrs. Raff could continue to live in the style to which her late husband had accustomed her. It astounded Alyssa that her mother could have been so foolish as to think that anyone could prevail upon His Lordship to give his detested former daughter-in-law a groat. But Mrs. Raff was an exceedingly foolish woman.

Although she was in no immediate danger of debtors' prison, she would be soon if her extravagances were not curbed and her finances put on a more solid basis. Alyssa set about doing this. Mrs. Raff, eager to escape the bill collectors who were constantly pounding upon her door, was only too happy to turn her financial affairs over to Alyssa until she arranged to sell Mrs. Raff's big house in Bloomsbury for a handsome profit. The furious widow agreed to the sale only after her late husband's solicitor warned her bluntly that if she did not do so, she would indeed find herself in debtors' prison before long. Alyssa used the proceeds to pay her mama's debts and to buy her this much more modest dwelling in a less expensive neighborhood. The remainder Alyssa invested in the funds to supplement Mrs. Raff's tiny income.

With the large house went the expense of its large staff of servants that had been such an enormous drain on Mrs. Raff's meager income. Alyssa's success in untangling and improving her mama's finances earned her no gratitude from Mrs. Raff, who complained bitterly about each and every one of her daughter's economies. But Mrs. Raff, like Lord Eliot before her, discovered that Alyssa could be a strong, determined woman who would not be swayed from a necessary path either by the bluster and threats that her grandfather employed or by the whining and cajoling her mama used.

Alyssa rolled over on the bed and stared up at the ceiling. Her only reward for helping her mother was the knowledge that if Mrs. Raff would be frugal, she could easily live within her modest income. But frugality was foreign to the widow's nature, and Alyssa's efforts to run a prudent household brought her nothing but an unending stream of complaints from her spendthrift parent and half sister that she was excessively clutch-fisted.

Tears trickled down Alyssa's cheeks. How she wished that she could return to Northumberland.

At Vauxhall Gardens, Mrs. Raff and Rosina promenaded down the long, arched gallery and across the large square dominated by the orchestra, which was accompanying a buxom soprano of impressive range. Mrs. Raff quickly ascertained that she was quite the most richly dressed woman there. All the others looked so insipid in muslin gowns like those Alyssa favored. Even their hair was insipid, worn unpowdered in flat curls about their faces instead of in the grand manner that she had chosen.

On the other side of the square, illuminated by festoons of colored lights suspended from elms and poplars, she guided her daughter past the boxes where the fashionable sat to sup and enjoy the entertainment. Mrs. Raff was well pleased by the number of stares that she drew from the boxes and fancied that once she was established as the marquess of Stanwood's mother-in-law, she would quickly become the leader of fashion.

And she was determined that she would become his mother-in-law. Even though Alyssa was too sapskulled to appreciate her good fortune, her mama was not. Mrs. Raff, who had twice snapped the parson's mousetrap shut on unwilling men, was now determined to do the same for her elder daughter whether the vexingly stupid girl wanted it or not. There was, after all, a duke to be gotten for Rosina and a widowed lord for herself.

Since the marquess had made his offer, Mrs. Raff had thought of nothing else but how best to ensure that the wedding took place. She was particularly alarmed by Alyssa's foolish insistence that the betrothal be kept a secret, thereby leaving the way open for the marquess to try to wriggle off the hook.

His father, Mrs. Raff had decided, would likely be the most difficult hurdle, just as Lord Eliot had been to her own first marriage. The duke would have to be put on notice that Mrs. Raff and her daughter were not women to be trifled with. If his son did not stand by his promise, Mrs. Raff would create a magnificent public scandal. Although Alyssa had warned that the duke would care naught, her mama was certain that her daughter had windmills in her head. Mrs. Raff remembered with satisfaction that even the recalcitrant Lord Eliot had given way before the scandal broth that she had brewed when he had refused permission for his son to marry her. Of course, the old tyrant had then been so disobliging as to disinherit his son, but Mrs. Raff did not think that the duke would do that to the marquess, for unlike Lord Eliot, he had no other son.

"La, Mama, look at that man over there," Rosina said. "Ain't he the thing, though."

Mrs. Raff, glancing in the direction that her daughter had indicated, beheld a man so handsome that her aging heart beat faster. He had an aristocratic face with luminous eyes beneath thick dark brows, and he moved with fluid, arrogant grace. The quiet elegance of his clothes quite put in the shade the other, more ostentatiously dressed men in his vicinity. So commanding was his presence that he had drawn the attention of several parties standing near Mrs. Raff, and she heard a woman in one of them exclaim, "Who is that dashing man?"

"None other than the duke of Carlyle himself," her gentleman companion answered.

"So that is Carlyle!" the woman exclaimed. "But he is so young. From all the tales they tell of him, I would have thought him older."

Mrs. Raff stared in admiration at Alyssa's future father-in-law. Suddenly, her quest for a widowed lord became more specific and lofty. If her prim, scrawny daughter could snare his son, surely a clever woman of her own voluptuous charms could win the father, who was as prime an article as Mrs. Raff had ever seen. She smoothed the wide skirt of her red satin gown with hands whose every finger was beringed, patted her soaring coiffure, and again congratulated herself on being the best-dressed woman at Vauxhall. What a rare piece of luck, she thought. The duke could not help but be impressed when she introduced herself to him.

His Grace of Carlyle cordially disliked Vauxhall Gardens, but he had come because he had been informed that Lord Rudolph Oldfield—whom he disliked even more than Vauxhall—was there tonight. Oldfield, the most malicious gossip in London, could be counted upon to recall in awesome detail every shocking scandal and immoral liaison that had occurred among the ton during the past two decades. He would surely know under whose protection Miss Raff had lived during those years that she had been absent from her parents' house.

The duke, spotting Oldfield's portly figure moving through the light-festooned square, sauntered casually up and greeted him with feigned surprise. His Lordship, fancying himself a pink of the ton, dressed with a foppish ostentation that Carlyle loathed, but the duke was careful to hide his distaste for both the man and his clothes behind a screen of inconsequential conversation.

Although His Grace detested gossip, he exchanged *on-dits* with Oldfield for several minutes before casually introducing Miss Raff's name into the conversation. "I see Lord Palmer over there with a new beauty on his arm. Wasn't he the one who sported that exquisite bit of muslin named Raff a couple of years ago? I wonder what has happened to her?"

"Raff?" Oldfield was perplexed. "I don't recall any cyprian by that name."

"I believe her given name was Alyssa."

"An unusual name, one I would surely remember, and I have never heard of an Alyssa Raff," Oldfield said with certainty. "The only woman named Alyssa that I know lives in Northumberland and is as proper a lady of quality as you would ever want to meet."

"Then why would I want to meet her?" the duke queried mockingly.

Oldfield laughed so long and loudly at this sally that His Grace, who knew that Oldfield could recite the long list of Carlyle's dalliances without skipping a single one, heartily regretted having made it.

Taking his leave of Oldfield, the duke pondered why the old gossip had never heard of the Raff woman. It must mean that she had lived abroad with her protector.

Carlyle strode across the square to return to the landing dock when he saw bearing down upon him two women of such stunning vulgarity that it momentarily checked him. The younger was poured into a purple satin gown that, even in this day of low-cut bodices, still revealed more décolletage than the duke had seen outside of a boudoir or a bordello. Although some men might have found the girl attractive, her petulant eyes, pouting face, and overblown body that would run to fat by the time she was five-and-twenty were not at all to the duke's notoriously exacting taste.

The older woman with her was undoubtedly a bawdy house proprietor out advertising one of her wares. She had her hair—and clearly a good deal of someone else's as well—done up in a coiffure that in height and stability reminded him of the Leaning Tower at Pisa. Her garish gown of vivid red satin was as outmoded as her hairstyle. But what most astonished His Grace was the remarkable quantity of tawdry paste jewelry that she had contrived to hang upon her person.

He was understandably thunderstruck when these visions of vulgarity accosted him. Surely, he did not look like a customer for the wares they were peddling.

"La, Your Grace," said the elder of the two, who looked to be fifty, flourishing her fan of painted vellum and tortoiseshell as coyly and coquettishly as an innocent eighteen-year-old maiden, "I'm monstrously happy to see you."

"I fear that I cannot return that sentiment," His Grace said in his most freezing manner. "Who are you?"

His haughty coldness chilled the bold harpy into fluttering her fan nervously. "La, sir, though we have never met before, we are soon to be related." Her shrill voice was as ungenteel as her dress. "I am Mrs. Elias Raff— Fanny to you—and this is my younger daughter, Rosina."

For the second time that day the duke of Carlyle, famed for his sharp and ready tongue, was rendered speechless. Until now, he had thought his son an innocent, naive stripling ensnared by a beautiful conniving cyprian, but as he stared at her horrifyingly vulgar mother and sister, he sincerely wondered whether Jeremy was a candidate for Bedlam. Good God, was his son such a flat he could not recognize them for what they were?

Mrs. Raff, apparently mistaking Carlyle's shocked silence for surprise at news of his son's engagement, said, "Surely the marquess has told you that he is about to marry my daughter."

"My son, the marquess," said the duke through clenched teeth, "can marry no one without my permission until he reaches his majority, which is two years away."

Mrs. Raff forgot her fan and drew herself up indignantly. "I will not permit your son to use and abandon my daughter," the affronted mama cried dramatically. "He—and you as well—will learn to your sorrow that he cannot trifle with my innocent daughter's honor and not pay the piper."

The duke's thick, dark brows snapped together in a fearsome scowl, and his eyes glittered with such anger that the mother instinctively drew back from him in fear. So threatening scandal was to be the Raffs' game, was it? Anyone who was in the least acquainted with Carlyle could have told them it was a game they were bound to lose. He snapped, "No innocent, honorable twenty-five-year-old woman seeks to shackle a calfling."

"He made her a promise," Mrs. Raff persisted. "He will marry her or I will create the scandal of the century."

"You may create the scandal of the millennium for all that I care! I would consider it a very small price to pay for my son's escaping the clutches of the likes of you and your daughter."

The duke garnered small pleasure from the startled, crestfallen look in the woman's eyes. It was a moment before she could recover her nerve sufficiently to say, "I will not permit you to insult me."

"I will do far more than insult you! Any effort to trap my son will gain you only excessive grief." Although the duke's eyes were blazing with fury, his tone was as cold as death. "Perhaps you are not familiar with the laws on extortion. I am a very powerful man, and if you attempt to extort my son into marrying your daughter, I swear to you that I will see you in Newgate. Do not think for a moment that you will escape my vengeance."

The woman's bravado crumpled before the harsh, determined set of his face that confirmed he would carry out his vow as surely as the sun rose in the east. Her body sagged like a garish rag doll that had lost its stuffing. The startled fear in her eyes assured Carlyle that she would not dare to carry out her threats.

He whirled and strode furiously off. A union with that

wretched creature's daughter would mean only unmitigated misery for Jeremy, and the duke would prevent it, no matter what! And he would destroy Miss Alyssa Raff and her disgusting mother in the bargain.

Chapter 5

After a restless night the duke, who, like his son, preferred the country to the city, awoke early and decided upon a quiet ride in the park before anyone would be about.

The morning was gray and unseasonably cold. The rain had come during the night, turning the paths in the park to mud. As he rode the big sleek black that he used when he was in London, the duke, normally a keen observer of nature, was so preoccupied with thoughts of his son and the two vulgar trollops who had accosted him at Vauxhall the previous night that he scarcely noticed the dripping trees and the fog—sometimes thick, sometimes thin and wispy—that swirled about the horse chestnuts and hawthorns. Even the cascading golden splendor of a Scotch laburnum tree did not elicit his admiration. What did finally capture his eye, however, was a young woman on a spirited chestnut hack with a groom trailing behind her at a respectful distance.

Her demeanor and the tailoring of her riding habit, although not the very latest style, proclaimed her to be a lady of quality. Yet London's fashionable ladies did not quit their beds until the day was much farther advanced than this. Furthermore, His Grace appreciated good horsemanship, whether the rider be male or female, and this woman had as good a seat as he had ever seen among her sex. As she stopped her hack by the golden glory of the laburnum and dismounted, he saw that she was strikingly lovely. Although she was tall, she made no attempt to minimize her height as a more self-conscious woman might have done, but instead carried herself with proud dignity. Her riding habit revealed a slender, beautifully proportioned body. Carlyle reined up not far from where she stood by the tree. Rich auburn hair, sparkling with reddish-gold lights in the morning sun, framed her delicate face with its beguiling dimple in the cleft of her chin.

Becoming aware of his bold stare, she turned her green eyes to him, meeting his with a curious and unflinchingly direct gaze that was not in the slightest nervous or coy or flirtatious. After a moment of mutual contemplation, the intrigued duke flashed her his most seductive smile. Immediately, the emerald eyes became frosty. She tilted her head back in an unconsciously regal rejection of his overture, remounted her chestnut hack, and rode off.

He smiled appreciatively at the silent, queenly setdown that she had given him. Rarely were the duke of Carlyle's overtures repulsed, but he was not in the least affronted that she had done so. Instead, she piqued both his interest and his curiosity. What an uncommon woman, he thought, wondering who she could be. He did not recall ever having seen her in London society, yet clearly she was a lady of quality several years out of the schoolroom. Connoisseur that he was of female charms, he could not believe that he could have overlooked her.

Alyssa rode away from the golden laburnum without looking back at the man on the magnificent black. It was his horse that first caught her eye, but it was immediately forgotten in favor of its owner. Alyssa, an excellent rider herself, was impressed by how skillfully he handled his difficult mount. However, it was his arresting eyes beneath thick, dark brows, rather than the handsome face in which

41

they were set or his equestrian ability, that most fascinated her. She had no idea who he might be, although it was clear from the elegance of his clothes and the arrogance of his bearing that he was a gentleman of the first water. Yet he was riding at a shockingly early hour for a member of the London ton, and he was alone, without even a groom to attend him.

She had regarded him with her usual directness and curiosity, which clearly gave him the impression that she was a vulgarly forward woman, if not worse. For she recognized the invitation in his seductive smile for what it was and blamed her own want of conduct for erroneously convincing him that she was a bold, fast piece.

For some reason the idea that the stranger might think anything but the very best of her sorely distressed Alyssa. She was amazed that she should be so concerned about what a man thought of her. Certainly that had not been the case with any of her suitors. Poor things. She smiled at the memory. Her tyrannical grandfather, who preferred her company to that of any other member of his family, had been determined to keep her a spinster at his side. He had even denied her a London season to keep her from the attention of would-be suitors, but several persistent gentlemen had made their way to Ormandy Park. Three had even possessed sufficient courage and perseverance to ask her grandfather for her hand, but he had refused them all without so much as consulting her. Since none of the trio had won Alyssa's heart, she did not regret that Lord Eliot sent them packing, although she had argued violently with him for not consulting her before he did so.

If Alyssa could not find a man whom she loved, she preferred to remain with her grandfather. Mrs. Raff might scorn her daughter's romantic notions, but as far as Alyssa could see, neither of her mother's marriages had brought her much happiness. And, at least, Mama's husbands had treated her kindly. Alyssa had seen enough unloved wives, ignored or mistreated, to realize her mama had been fortunate in that respect. To Alyssa, the saddest example was the duchess of Berwick, one of the loveliest, gayest, most enchanting creatures that Alyssa had ever met. Before her marriage, they had been neighbors in Northumberland. A half dozen years older than Alyssa, Lady Selena Wright had been the incomparable of her first London season. Almost every eligible bachelor in England had been in hot pursuit of her until the duke of Berwick claimed her hand.

For Selena, it had been a love match as well as a brilliant marriage, but her duke did not return her affection. As that odious gossip, Lord Rudolph Oldfield, had once quipped, the duchess had won the heart of every man in the kingdom save one—her husband. Selena hid her pain at her husband's rejection behind a charming, madcap facade of extravagant gaiety. How any man could resist her was beyond Alyssa's comprehension, but the duke did.

In time, the despairing duchess sought solace for his neglect with other men. It was then that Lord Eliot, as high a stickler as ever there was when it came to morals, prohibited his granddaughter from any contact with Selena. Although he could stop Alyssa from seeing the disgraceful duchess, as he called her, he could not prevent his granddaughter's heart from aching for her. Alyssa was convinced that no fate could be more devastating than to be married to a man whom one loved wildly and not have that affection returned.

No, she would prefer her grandfather's company to a loveless marriage. She had been tolerably happy with him. He might be irascible, but he was not boring. Although the rest of Lord Eliot's family held him in the liveliest terror, Alyssa had never permitted him to cow her. Her spirit, coupled with her lively intelligence, had made her his favorite companion. Although she was a mere woman, he often paid her the compliment of arguing his ideas and his conclusions with her before setting them down in the distinguished histories that had won him much acclaim. How Alyssa yearned now for those discussions, for Ormandy Park, and for the neighbors there, especially Lady Braden and her daughter, Letitia.

A minishower cascaded down on Alyssa as she rode beneath the wet leaves of a horse chestnut tree's spreading branches, and one large drop hit the tip of her nose. She looked over her shoulder at Oliver's young groom, who was following her at a respectful distance. Oliver insisted that the lad accompany her whenever she rode. She agreed to this, although she privately thought that the dull, rawboned youth of eighteen, who had not yet been properly trained, was of little use.

The fog was growing thicker, obscuring the dripping trees and giving them an eerie, ethereal appearance, and Alyssa did not notice the tiny figure that darted out of the milky mist as she trotted by. With an unintelligible cry, it grabbed at the skirt of her riding habit.

This unexpected assault from the side frightened her high-strung chestnut, and he reared violently. Suddenly Alyssa was fighting to retain her seat, control the frightened animal, and keep his plunging hooves from striking the child, who stood rooted by terror instead of attempting to dodge away.

To her horror, although she heard no impact of hoof against flesh and bone, she saw the little boy fall unconscious to the muddy ground.

Alyssa, struggling desperately, at last imposed her will on the rearing chestnut and managed to quiet him as the big black she had seen earlier galloped up, its rider dismounting even before it stopped beside her.

She found herself staring down into hazel eyes flecked with gold, set in a classically handsome face, with its straight nose and strong jaw. The penetrating eyes with their heavy brows made their owner seem a little frightening despite the concern that she saw in them. Tall, lean, and impeccably garbed in a russet green riding coat, snowy white neckcloth, pristine buckskin breeches, and jackboots that had been polished to a high gloss, he moved with a singular grace. From a distance his trim body and thick crop of dark, curly hair had misled Alyssa into thinking him to be about her own age, but now she saw that he was a few years older.

"Are you hurt?" he asked, anxiety in his soft voice.

"No," Alyssa replied. Among her family, she was known for her ability to maintain a levelheaded poise in any emergency. Although now she was much shaken by what had occurred, she retained an outwardly calm demeanor.

He asked mockingly, "What, no hysterics?"

"I have no time to waste on such nonsense." Her contempt for this weakness was apparent in her tone. "That poor child needs help."

The newcomer cast a fulminating glance at Oliver Hagar's groom, who had made no attempt to come to her aid but had watched with slack-jawed paralysis as she struggled with the chestnut. "That fool is of no use whatsoever," the stranger snapped, helping her to dismount.

She ran to the child, who was lying faceup on the muddy path, his head resting in a rut where an inch of coffee-colored water had collected. A sturdy-looking boy with blond curls and a cherubic face, he was wearing a nankeen jacket over a flannel nightshirt that reached to his ankles. His feet were encased in low top boots with silver tassels, and a nightcap lay in the water beside his head. The top button of the jacket, which was in the second buttonhole, thereby throwing off the entire sequence, gave mute testimony to having been hastily fastened by inexperienced fingers. From the child's size, she guessed him to be about three years old.

Alyssa was no novice to injury and illness. Her skill in treating both was widely respected in Northumberland.

From her old Welsh nurse, she had learned a great deal about herb medicines and folk remedies that were often more effective than the leeches and bleeding that were inevitably the physician's prescription, and many in the neighborhood around Ormandy Park preferred Miss Eliot to a doctor when sickness struck them. Now she knelt in the mud beside the unconscious little boy.

The stranger dropped to his knee on the other side of the fallen child, saying, "Let me attend to him. You will ruin your skirt in the mud."

"How can you think that I care about my skirt when this poor child is hurt?" she demanded indignantly, stripping off her leather riding gloves.

Although she was reluctant to move the boy until she had ascertained what injuries he might have suffered, she slid her fingers into the muck beneath his blond head and eased it from the water in the rut. When she removed her hands after performing this task, they were dripping with mud. She looked about helplessly for something to wipe them on and was about to resort to the already soiled skirt of her riding habit when her companion thrust at her a spotless white handkerchief of the finest linen embroidered with the initial *R*.

She drew back at the thought of dirtying it, saying, "I could not use—"

"Don't be silly," he cut her off, seizing her right hand, then her left, in his and wiping the muck from them as though she were a recalcitrant child. Although his fingers were brisk and impersonal as they went about their task, his touch sent a frisson of excitement along her spine. By the time he finished with both her hands, the fine handkerchief was a muddy ruin. Meanwhile, Oliver's young groom stood a few feet away, gaping at the strange tableau in motionless wonder.

Alyssa began to check the boy for injuries. There was no blood, nor could she see any other sign of a wound inflicted by the chestnut's hooves. Moving expertly over his body, her hands searched for injuries.

Her companion, who was watching her actions intently, said musingly, "You seem to know what you are doing."

"I am thought to be a tolerably good nurse," she said coolly, without looking up from her task. Finally, unable to find any obvious injury on the little body, she told her companion so.

The man nodded. "I am convinced that he fainted from fright. Where are your smelling salts?"

"I don't carry any."

Her companion said mockingly, "But what if you should faint?"

His tone, tinged with a sarcasm that bespoke his contempt for her sex, rankled her, and she said with asperity, "I have never fainted in my life, nor do I intend to."

Amusement flickered in his gold-flecked eyes. "I admire a woman of resolve."

The irony in his tone did not escape her, and she studied him for a moment with her frank, curious gaze. "I collect that you do not admire women at all."

The hazel eyes widened in surprise. "No, I do not," he admitted candidly, "although I must congratulate you on a remarkable piece of horsemanship in keeping your seat and your chestnut from annihilating this child."

"I am thought to be a tolerably good horsewoman."

"Your modesty is commendable. You are superb."

Alyssa found herself inordinately pleased by his compliment.

He asked, "Do you ride often here in the park?"

"Daily. And you?"

"Frequently, when I am in London," he replied, removing his russet green riding coat. It was so superbly cut and tailored that Alyssa knew only the incomparable Weston could have produced such a fine garment. Walking a few feet from the muddy path, he spread it on the wet grass.

"What are you doing?" she demanded, shocked by his careless treatment of such an expensive garment.

"I'm going to wrap the child in it." As he spoke, he was undoing his neckcloth of starched white muslin that had been tied with superb style. "That light jacket is not warm enough for him. Even if it were, it is wet from the puddle of water he fell into. Lying like that on the cold, damp ground will do him no good."

Alyssa stared in dismay at the beautiful coat and then at the muddy child. "But it will be ruined," she protested, "and it is far too costly and fine."

"How can you think that I care about my coat when this poor child is hurt?" he said, teasingly repeating her earlier question.

Alyssa began unbuttoning her own jacket, which was inferior in fabric and tailoring to his.

"What the devil are you doing?" he demanded abruptly.

"We will use my jacket and spare your beautiful coat," she said crisply.

He gave her an odd look that she could not decipher and said irritably, "Do not be a shatterbrain. The morning is much too chilly for you to give it up."

"But—"

"Do as I say," he ordered in a voice that brooked no opposition. Clearly, he was a man who was used to issuing commands and having them obeyed.

"You are odiously commanding!" she retorted, rebuttoning her jacket.

He grinned, and the smile banished the harsh cynicism from his face, making him look almost boyish and causing Alyssa's heart to skip a beat. Amusement became him.

"So I have been told," he said cheerfully. "Your wardrobe will be the better for it, even if you are not properly grateful."

Kneeling again beside the little boy, he lifted the limp little body from the muddy path and carried him to the coat. Before wrapping him in it, he dried the boy's wet hair and wiped the worst of the mud from him, using his fine muslin neckcloth as a towel. When he finished, the muslin was as soiled as his linen handkerchief. Looking up at Alyssa with a smile so warm and full of laughter that her heart thumped wildly, he said in amusement, "I do hope that there are no more runaway children about the park this morning. I am running out of clothes.

He removed the child's wet nankeen jacket and gently wrapped him, still clad in his flannel nightgown and low top boots, in the warmth of the exquisite russet green coat.

Initially, Alyssa had been dismayed by her companion's clear disdain for her sex, but now, having seen how carefully and gently he had handled the unconscious child, she found herself liking him more by the minute. "Where can he have come from?" she asked.

"His odd attire tells me he is a nursery escapee out for a morning fling."

"What shall we do with him?"

The boy groaned, and his eyelids fluttered.

"He's coming round," her companion said. "I am hoping that when he regains his senses, we can prevail upon him to lead us to his home."

Opening his eyes, the child looked blurrily up at them, trying to focus. When he could make out the two strangers kneeling over him, he began to sob in fright. Alyssa's companion lifted him, still wrapped in the russet green coat, into his arms and comforted the crying boy with soft, soothing words until his panic subsided.

When the boy was quieted, the man, still holding him in his arms, asked softly, "What is your name?"

"Oo-ses."

"Oo-ses," Alyssa repeated blankly.

"Eustice," translated her companion with a mischievous grin at Alyssa.

The child broke into a wide smile. "That's right. Oo-ses."

"Eustice, I am Richard."

So that was what the embroidered *R* on the handkerchief stood for, Alyssa thought.

"Where do you live, Eustice?" Richard asked.

The boy's face clouded. "It gone away."

"Your home has gone away?" Richard asked.

Eustice nodded and, between increasingly loud and frequent sniffles, poured out a disjointed and at times not very intelligible story.

From it, however, his adult companions were able to glean that while his nursemaid had been occupied with his baby sister, he had slipped from his nursery, down the steps, and, in the light of dawn, out the front door to the park across the street, where he loved to play. Only this morning, the fog had descended upon him. Disoriented by it, he had been unable to find his way back home. Worse, the park had been deserted, and Alyssa had been the first person he had seen. In his panic, he had dashed at her as she rode by and grabbed for her skirts.

"My 'ome ran away," Eustice concluded, his sniffles becoming full-fledged tears.

"Eustice," Richard told him gravely, "I thought you had more bottom than to cry over such a paltry thing as a runaway house. Don't you know that, unlike horses, they never run far. We shall have no trouble finding it for you."

The boy's blue eyes, filled with tears, blinked. "Is you telling me a w'isker?"

"I don't tell whiskers," Richard denied, only the slightest twitching at the corner of his lips betraying his indignant tone. "Now describe your runaway home for me so that I shall know what to search for."

Eustice started to comply when out of the swirling fog

an apparition descended upon them, shrieking at the top of her very strong lungs. She was a thin stalk of a woman with a cap crazily askew upon uncombed straw-colored hair that protruded out from under it at odd and recalcitrant angles. Wrapped in a shapeless old cloak, she carried a bundle shrouded in blankets in her arms. From the wild look in her eyes she appeared to be demented.

Eustice turned his face to Richard and said in a tone that was a mixture of childish disgust and mischief, "That's my nursemaid, Pease. Let's run away from her."

"You've done quite enough running away already this morning," Richard told him sternly.

Seeing Richard with Eustice in his arms, Pease screamed, "Help, kidnappers! Master Eustice is being kidnapped."

As her shrill voice grew more loudly frantic, increasingly lusty wails rose from the bundle in her arms.

Trying to calm the woman, Alyssa said, "I assure you that this man is not a kidnapper."

She might as well have saved her breath. The woman eyed her wildly and shrieked, "And *you* are his accomplice!"

"Woman, quiet yourself!" Richard commanded in a voice of such frigidity and authority that Pease's shrieks died in her throat. "Do I look like a kidnapper?"

Alyssa smothered her laughter. Minus his stock and elegant jacket, his white shirt muddied from holding the dirty child, his thick, dark brows knit together in irritation, Alyssa thought that if not a kidnapper, certainly a buccaneer.

"No, sir," whimpered the discomforted Pease, belatedly recognizing aristocratic consequence, even though it came in a disreputable-looking package. Realizing her error, she launched into an incoherent explanation made all the more unintelligible by the lusty laments from the bundle in her arms, but Alyssa caught some phrases: "baby teething . . . naughty Eustice . . . always running away . . . the death of me yet."

Richard set Eustice upon the ground. Which was a mistake. The boy took advantage of his release to drop the russet green coat that had been wrapped around him into the mud and to flee as fast as his fat little legs could carry him across the wet grass, his nightshirt flapping above his top boots.

"Come back!" the nursemaid shrieked, running after him after shoving her blanketed bundle at Oliver's startled groom, who was standing like a gape-mouthed statue. The youth looked as though the nurse had thrust a savage beast into his arms and would have dropped the baby had Richard not had the quick presence of mind to snatch it from him.

"Good God," he demanded of the groom, "have you never handled a baby before?"

"Nay, sir."

The infant, clearly much frightened by the cavalier handling, was screaming in distress. Richard placed the squalling mite against his shoulder with a casual assurance that told Alyssa this was not the first time he had done so and comforted the baby with such skill that she soon stopped crying.

Alyssa watched with astonishment. None of the men of her acquaintance would have had the slightest idea of what to do with a baby, and she could not help being amused by the incongruous sight of this aristocratic man standing casually, without a trace of self-consciousness, in the middle of the park quieting an infant at his shoulder.

A teasing smile played on her lips. "Unlike my groom, sir, you are a great deal of use, especially with babies. How did you become so adept at handling them?"

He replied carelessly, "The usual way: two of my own and a passel of younger brothers and sisters."

A sudden sharp pain stabbed Alyssa's heart as she realized that he was married. Why should you have supposed he was not? she asked herself furiously and decided that it had been his contempt for women that had misled her. She wondered whether his wife was responsible for his attitude toward women.

"You look surprised," he commented.

"Most of the fathers of my acquaintance wish nothing to do with their squalling infants and have no more experience at handling them than that groom."

"They miss a great deal," he said quietly, looking across the grass toward Eustice.

The nursemaid had finally caught the runaway boy and was attempting to drag him back across the grass, but he had stubbornly dug in his heels and was resisting fiercely. Suddenly, he managed to break free from her grasp and turned to flee.

"Eustice, come here at once!" Richard called to him in a tone that demanded acquiescence.

The recalcitrant child, recognizing the voice of implacable authority, turned back and ran obediently to Richard, Pease at his heels.

Richard gestured toward his horse. "Would you like to ride with me while we find your runaway home?"

Eustice jumped up and down with excitement. "Oh, yes!"

The man handed the baby to the nurse. The infant, who had been contentedly sucking her thumb while in his arms, began to cry again.

As Richard lifted Eustice into the big black's saddle, Alyssa rescued his coat from the grass. The once spotless garment was wet and badly stained from the grass and mud. Its silk lining was soiled from contact with Eustice's muddy form. She brushed vigorously at it, but it was beyond her ability to do much good.

"I fear your beautiful coat is ruined," she said.

He shrugged as if it were of no consequence, took it from her, and mounted behind Eustice.

"Now, Pease," he told the nurse who was trying in vain

to quiet the crying baby, "if you will hand me the infant and be so good to lead the way, we shall take these children home."

The woman, by now thoroughly cowed by his autocratic authority, obeyed.

"Let me get my horse and go with you," Alyssa exclaimed. "I can carry the baby."

"No!" Richard said so sharply that she jumped.

"Why not?"

"Consider what an odd spectacle we should make, riding in the park like a mother and father with their two small children at an unheard-of early hour. I am very well known. If anyone were to see us, it would undoubtedly start unfortunate rumors."

Two dots of bright color rose in Alyssa's cheeks, but her voice was calm. "I see. You fear I would be thought to be your mistress and the children two of your by-blows."

He grinned at her. "Are you always so blunt?"

"Yes," she replied serenely. "I have often been told it is one of my great failings."

"I see," he said gravely, his lip quavering. "You do not seem overly concerned about your great failing."

"No, for I do not consider forthrightness a failing. I shall remain here while you leave. I should not like to damage your reputation."

"Paperskull!" he exclaimed. "I don't care about my reputation. It is yours that concerns me!" He turned to the nurse. "Lead the way."

The strange procession set off, the nurse guiding them on foot and the man following atop his big black, Eustice in front of him and the baby nestled in one arm.

Alyssa watched until they had vanished from sight. What a singular man Richard was. She had been impressed by his expert handling of Eustice and his baby sister. What an excellent husband and father he must be. Initially she had been disturbed by his cynical mockery, but once that had given way to concern and then amusement, she had been charmed by him.

But he had not been sufficiently curious about her even to ask her name. For some reason, that omission stung her painfully.

Chapter 6

Alyssa would have been gratified to know that, contrary to what she thought, the stranger rode away from their encounter in the park every bit as curious about her identity as she was about his. But Carlyle had deliberately not asked her name, knowing that this omission would pique her. Since she rode every morning in the park, he would know where to find her and would have ample opportunity to learn who she was.

As he sat down to a breakfast delayed by the necessity of restoring Eustice to his runaway home, the duke was much amused by the morning's unexpected adventure and much intrigued by the lady of the laburnum, as he had dubbed her.

When he had first seen her, he had thought her uncommon. Now he thought her unique: No other woman of his acquaintance could have retained her seat on that rearing, plunging horse and brought him under control as she had done. But more remarkable still was her calm during the crisis. Most women would have dissolved in strong hysterics, thereby turning a dangerous situation into a disaster for both the child and herself.

He remembered her indignation when he teased her about fainting and smelling salts. Remembered, too, her concern for the unconscious child lying on the ground. Carlyle thought of her kneeling in the muddy path beside Eustice, heedless of the damage to her skirt, as she removed his head from the muddy puddle. His Grace had been touched by her willingness, despite the cold of the morning, to shed her own jacket to spare his coat. A smile, free of his usual cynicism when he contemplated women, curled the duke's lips.

When she had stripped off her gloves to help the boy, he had hastily checked for a wedding ring and was surprised to see that she was not married. Lack of dowry undoubtedly was responsible for a woman of such beauty, breeding, and calm good sense being on the shelf. Her candor and humor had delighted as well as surprised him. Although she was clearly a lady of propriety, she was not missish or she would not have used words like mistress and by-blow so frankly.

He suspected she was too proper a lady to indulge in an affair, but perhaps she could be persuaded. Women came so easily to his bed that it would be a novel experience to be rebuffed. He wondered if, in the end, after she learned his own identity, she would have the strength of character to resist him or whether she, too, would be seduced by his title and fortune.

The door opened and Jeremy came in. His father's pleasant thoughts of spirited emerald eyes were instantly replaced by the decidedly unpleasant memories of two garishly dressed harpies at Vauxhall Gardens. After meeting them, Carlyle's sympathy for Jeremy's puppy love had faded. His Grace could not fathom how the boy could have developed a tendre for such a vulgar creature as Alyssa Raff must surely be.

After exchanging greetings with his father, Jeremy turned to the sideboard and began filling his breakfast plate with a generosity that demonstrated love had not affected his healthy appetite.

His Grace wondered what Miss Raff would tell his son

about his confrontation with her mother at Vauxhall. She would, of course, attempt to portray him in the worst possible light, making much of his threats. But she had been so adamant about keeping the betrothal from him that it would be embarrassing for her to have to admit that her own mother had told him.

Clearly there was a sharp difference of opinion between mother and daughter on the most effective tactic to be used in shackling Jeremy. The mother had thought to seal the nuptials by broadcasting the betrothal and threatening scandal; the daughter had sought to keep it a secret. But why? Without his father's permission, Jeremy could not wed for two years, and Miss Raff must know that the duke would never give it. Nor could she hope to keep the boy infatuated until he reached his majority. Carlyle was more convinced than ever that she hoped to persuade Jeremy to elope to Gretna Green.

The only other possibility was that she thought the duke would quietly buy her off for an extortionate sum. To deliberately take this sweet, naive calfling's heart and break it for financial gain, leaving him humiliated and disillusioned, seemed to Carlyle cruel beyond belief. He wanted to curse the greedy hussy aloud as he studied Jeremy's happy, open face across the table from him. If ever that conniving Jezebel dared solicit him to buy her off, he would wring her vicious neck.

He intended to serve immediate notice on the vulgar trollop that regardless of whether elopement was her strategy or whether she hoped to exact payment from him for breaking the betrothal, she would gain nothing—and would lose much—if she pursued either course. Once she learned that, she would move on to more lucrative and less dangerous prospects.

His Grace longed to tell his son what a shocking lack of both sense and taste he had demonstrated by offering for such a creature. But to do so would only make Jeremy more stubbornly defensive of his vulgar choice. So when Carlyle spoke, it was in a deceptively languid voice. "I confess to having succumbed to an overwhelming desire to see your divine Alyssa. If I go to Almack's tonight, will you point her out to me?"

"She . . . she won't be there. She is going to a party."

"Does she not have vouchers to Almack's?" Carlyle asked, certain that the only entry Miss Alyssa Raff enjoyed was to certain establishments of ill-repute in Covent Garden.

Jeremy blushed. "No," he admitted.

"I rather suspected as much after meeting her mama and sister at Vauxhall last night."

Jeremy choked on the egg he was eating, and the duke observed that his blush grew even deeper. Clearly the boy was not blind to the excessive vulgarity of the Raffs. But why, then, if he saw them for what they were, had he made his offer?

When Jeremy recovered himself sufficiently to speak, he stammered, "How did you come to meet them?"

"Mrs. Raff introduced herself because she wished to inform me of your betrothal. I found her eagerness for me to know of it curious in light of her daughter's reluctance." Carlyle leaned back in his chair and regarded his son, who stared at him in silent surprise. "Mrs. Raff seems quite certain that you are merely toying with her daughter's affections and will soon try to cry off the betrothal. It pains me to tell you that she made some ugly threats about intending to force you to the altar with her daughter, whether you wish to go or not."

Jeremy's obstinacy was immediately raised by Mrs. Raff's threats, as Carlyle had known it would be. "That woman cannot force me to do anything!" the youth cried indignantly.

"Of course not," his father said soothingly. "I assured her that if you should decide against marrying her daughter, nothing she could do would induce you to do so and she would be a fool to try.''

''She is an excessively vulgar, odious woman!''

''I noticed,'' the duke said dryly.

Jeremy's color deepened. ''Be assured, Papa, that Alyssa is nothing like her mother.''

Carlyle was far from assured, but he said blandly, ''I am relieved. I must confess to having had some qualms after meeting her mother and sister.''

''You will see at a glance that Alyssa is a lady of quality!''

His Grace was certain that Miss Raff was neither lady nor quality. He had known other cyprians whose wealthy lovers had managed to give them a veneer of polish and sophistication. But beneath it, Miss Raff would be as vulgar and grasping as her relatives, and he would have to find a way to show his son this. ''What party is Miss Raff attending tonight?''

''Oliver Hagar's,'' Jeremy replied.

''Hagar? I do not recognize the name.''

''He is an aide to the first minister. It is at his house that I met Alyssa.''

''How do you know him?''

''He and his wife are acquaintances of Uncle Sidney. He took me to their house while you were at Beauchamp.''

The duke silently cursed both his youngest brother and the unknown Oliver Hagar for their contribution to his son's besotted state.

''The Hagars give such bang-up parties,'' Jeremy said enthusiastically. ''I know that you would enjoy them.''

''Then, by all means, I must sample one sometime,'' the duke said carelessly. He planned to do so that very night, but he did not tell Jeremy of his intention. He preferred to surprise Miss Raff.

Chapter 7

After returning Oliver's chestnut, Alyssa stopped to talk to Charlotte, her best friend and the only person to whom she dared confide the situation with Jeremy.

When Charlotte heard Alyssa's subtle strategy for dissuading him, she said frankly, "I know that you are too kindhearted to hurt the boy, but I don't like it. God help you if Carlyle ever finds out that you are supposedly betrothed to his son. He is a very powerful and dangerous enemy."

"I know, but he is at Beauchamp, and I am certain that I will get Jeremy to cry off before he can learn of it."

"I sincerely hope so," Charlotte replied, an uncharacteristic frown marring her lively face framed by a halo of brown curls. "Is Jeremy bringing you to my party tonight?"

"Yes, but remember our supposed betrothal is a secret."

"I won't tell," Charlotte said. "How was your ride this morning?"

Alyssa told her about her adventure with Eustice and Richard.

"How diverting!" Charlotte said when Alyssa concluded. "And how unfortunate that you did not learn Richard's identity. I have never before seen your eyes glow the way they did when you talked of him. Can it be that a man has finally pierced the armor of your heart?''

''Don't be silly,'' Alyssa exclaimed. ''He is married.'' If only he were not.

When Alyssa returned to her mother's house, she found a note had been delivered for her in her absence. Opening it, Alyssa discovered that it was from Lady Braden, who had come up to London only the day before with her two youngest children, Letitia and George, for a few weeks.

Lady Braden, a sensible, intelligent, plainspoken woman, was a favorite of Alyssa's. Since the death of Her Ladyship's husband two years ago, she had been living with her very elderly father whose property, Salis, adjoined Ormandy Park. Her late husband's modest estate in Berkshire had been inherited by her eldest son, whose wife was an ill-tempered, overbearing female, who had resented the establishment's former mistress's remaining there. So Lady Braden had left it for Salis with the two youngest of her six children: George, who was now twenty and helping to manage his ailing grandfather's estate, and seventeen-year-old Letty.

Alyssa was especially fond of Letty, a good-hearted, intelligent girl with a lively sense of humor. When she had first come to Salis, she had been more boy than girl, both in body and behavior. As the baby and only female among six children, she had been used to holding her own with big brothers and male playmates as she was growing up. A tall, thin stick of a girl, still awkward in her movements and embarrassed by her height, she had sought to disguise it by slouching.

After Letty's arrival at Salis, Alyssa took her in hand, encouraging her self-confidence and teaching her feminine poise. Seeing how straight and gracefully Alyssa, who was an inch taller than Letty, carried herself inspired the younger girl to mimic her graceful carriage. Alyssa had Letty's hair cut so that it curled softly about her face, accentuating its pixieish charm. By the time Alyssa left for London, Letty had been transformed from a plain girl to a very pretty young lady. If only Lady Braden had the resources to give her daughter a London coming out.

But knowing how limited those resources were, Alyssa was surprised to learn that she had come to London at all and wondered what had brought her. Her note gave no clue but begged Alyssa to call upon her as soon as possible. Delighted at the prospect of once again seeing her friends from Northumberland, Alyssa decided to do so that very afternoon.

Hugh Page, summoned to his employer's presence, found Carlyle pacing the floor of his book room, the sound of his footsteps deadened by the Aubusson rug on the floor. As Hugh closed the door behind him, he saw that the duke was seething.

"Good God, Hugh," Carlyle exclaimed, "when you told me how dreadful the Raffs were, I hoped you were overstating the situation. If anything, you understated it."

He described his meeting at Vauxhall with Mrs. Raff and Rosina, concluding, "I will do anything, anything at all, to prevent Jeremy from being shackled to that vulgar doxy. I must find a way to bring my son to his senses. It is not that I wish him to marry title and fortune—you know that."

Hugh did. His Grace had sanctioned love matches between two of his sisters and a brother, with spouses far inferior in wealth and social standing.

"I want only that Jeremy be happy." The duke was still pacing. "I want him to have a wife who truly loves him, who will be devoted to him and his children."

Such a wife, Hugh reflected, was what the duke himself had needed in his own marriage instead of the selfish princess that he had had foisted on him for diplomatic reasons.

"Jeremy is a born romantic and eager for a family of his own," the duke continued. "Having never been exposed to domestic strife, the poor boy cannot appreciate how unhappy the wrong wife will make him.''

There was such a wistful echo to Carlyle's tone that Hugh was certain His Grace was also thinking of his own marriage. The duke was silent for a moment before asking briskly, "Have you been able to discover who Miss Raff's protector was?''

"No, I have learned nothing more about her, only about her mother,'' Hugh replied. "Mrs. Raff's late husband was a wealthy merchant until she dissipated his fortune with her extravagances. Apparently, she fancied herself quite the grand lady, too far above her former neighbors to associate with them.''

"How fortunate for them! The vulgar harridan! Tonight I confront Miss Raff herself. I shall make it very clear to her that she will never enjoy the title and fortune that she hopes to gain by marrying Jeremy, even if it means I must disown him.''

Knowing how much Carlyle loved his son, Hugh exclaimed in disbelief, "Surely you would not do that!''

"But Miss Raff does not know that.''

"But she will tell Jeremy of your threat, and it is certain to cause a breach between you and him.''

The duke's mouth tightened in a grim line. "I am all too aware of that risk, but it is one I must take for my son's sake. I am not convinced that she will tell him. It would reveal the crass reason why she is crying off the betrothal. That would begin to open his eyes to her true character. I intend to open them even further by presenting him with proof of her past liaisons.''

"But we do not know who they were—or even whether she had more than one.''

"I rely upon you to see that we quickly acquire such information.''

Hugh instantly comprehended what the duke wanted of him. "I know of a former Bow Street Runner who is very good at such matters and handles them discreetly, but his price is high.''

"Employ him at once. I count any price that will save my son from that strumpet as cheap.''

By the time that Alyssa left for the Bradens', she was delighted to be escaping her mother's house, if only for a short time. Both Mrs. Raff and Rosina had been in sour humor all day, and Alyssa had not been able to get a word out of either as to what was wrong. Rosina walked about with a frightened look in her eyes. Mrs. Raff alternately whined about how cruel the world had been to her and snapped at the hapless maid-of-all-work and at her daughters, even at Rosina who normally could do no wrong in her mother's eyes. When Alyssa, seeking to divert her mama from her complaints, asked her how she had enjoyed Vauxhall the previous night, Mrs. Raff, who loved the pleasure garden, stigmatized it as a wretched place, not worth talking about.

When Alyssa reached the Bradens', she was led into a sitting room where a plump, motherly woman with graying hair hurried to greet her. Lady Braden hugged Alyssa warmly, exclaiming, "How good it is to see you again.''

Returning the embrace, Alyssa felt more welcome here than at her own mother's, especially today. "Are Letty and George here?''

"Unfortunately, no,'' Lady Braden said as she and Alyssa settled on a sofa. The room's furnishings, like those in many London lodgings for let, were more utilitarian than attractive. The brown sofa and two horsehair chairs of the same color were its only seats. "Letty has gone for a drive in the park this afternoon with a friend from Berkshire. She will be so disappointed when she learns that she missed you. And George has gone off with Lord Stanwood.''

"George knows Jeremy!'' Alyssa exclaimed.

"You've met His Lordship, then. Such a dear boy. My

late husband's land marched with Beauchamp, and Jeremy was like another brother to George and Letty."

Afraid that George might reveal her true name to Jeremy, Alyssa cried, "You must impress upon George that I am now known as Raff and he must never, ever, refer to me as Eliot to Jeremy or to anyone else in London. You know how adamant Grandpapa was that no one know I am an Eliot as long as I am residing with Mama."

Lady Braden sighed. "For a learned man, your grandpapa can be very foolish, but do not worry. I will make certain that George does not give you away. Your grandfather misses you, Alyssa."

"Enough to relent and let me return to Ormandy Park?"

"In time." Lady Braden squeezed Alyssa's hands comfortingly. "He was deeply hurt when you insisted on going to your mother, whom he detests. Now he is too proud and stubborn to admit that he wants nothing more than to have you at his side. Eventually he will come around."

But when? Alyssa wondered sadly. She desperately wanted to escape her mother's house, but until her grandfather took her back, she had nowhere to go.

"Be patient," Lady Braden counseled.

But it was not easy when Alyssa was so intensely unhappy beneath her mother's roof. "Does Grandpapa still plan to travel to Stockholm this summer?" she asked, remembering the other journeys that she had made with him in the past when he had been working on one or another of his histories. At various times, they had sojourned in Paris before the revolution, Rome, Venice, and Vienna.

"The journey has been postponed," Lady Braden replied. "I think that he does not want to travel without you. Your Northumberland neighbors miss you, too. Illness strikes with added terror, now that Miss Eliot cannot be summoned from Ormandy Park."

"You must not call me by that name," Alyssa cried in alarm.

"I won't again, I promise."

"What brings you to London?" Alyssa asked.

"George."

"I am surprised that you could tear him away from his beloved Sarah Turner. How unfortunate that her father died just as George was about to ask for her hand, or I imagine that they would be married."

"It appears now that they never will be," Lady Braden said.

"Why?" Alyssa demanded, much shocked. Although she privately thought Sarah Turner boring and insipid, she had rarely seen two young persons who seemed so much in love with each other as Sarah and George, who was not himself quick-witted.

"A few days after you left for London, Sarah's uncle and appointed guardian, Sir Egbert Turner, brought her here to live with him and his family."

"Her uncle is the most odious man, and that wife of his is even worse. Poor Sarah!" Alyssa exclaimed. "Don't tell me that the child has fallen in love with a London gentleman?"

Lady Braden shook her head sadly. "No, but she caught the fancy of Thomas Stokes, and her uncle insists that she marry him."

"That cruel, lecherous old reprobate!" Alyssa exclaimed in disgust. "Why, he is three times Sarah's age."

"That he is, but he is also rich as Midas, and Lord Turner is deep in dun territory. Poor George and Sarah love each other so, but His Lordship is unmoved by their pleas. George insisted upon coming to London to try to persuade her uncle to change his mind, but I am certain that his suit is hopeless."

"But that child cannot be permitted to marry Stokes. Sarah is scarcely out of the schoolroom, and he has already buried three wives. It is said that he helped them into their early graves by his cruel treatment." The thought of meek

67

little Sarah married to that dreadful old man made Alyssa ill. She understood, though, why Sarah would have caught Stokes's eye. The girl was as pretty as a picture with her blond curls and creamy complexion. But she was such a timid, spiritless, easily frightened little creature that Alyssa feared it would not be long before she shared the fate of Stokes's previous wives.

Lady Braden shrugged helplessly. "Her uncle insists that she marry him. What can George do to stop it?"

As Alyssa and Jeremy arrived for the Hagars' party that night, she saw at a glance that something was very wrong. Several guests had already arrived, but neither of the Hagars, usually the most attentive of hosts, had appeared to greet them. She asked where the couple was.

"The master, he went for a walk."

"With guests arriving!" Alyssa could not have been more surprised if the butler had said that Oliver, who had eyes for no woman but his beloved Charlotte, had eloped with a lightskirt.

"Yes, ma'am, and the mistress, she is feeling unwell. She wishes you to go to her immediately in her dressing room."

Alyssa, who had never known her vivacious hostess to be in anything but the best of health and spirits, was much alarmed. Hurrying upstairs, she found Charlotte lying, pale and listless, on a chaise.

"Whatever is the matter, Charlotte?"

"The duke of Carlyle is coming tonight."

"Here! But he is supposed to be at Beauchamp." The color drained from Alyssa's face. "Can it be possible that he knows about . . ." Her voice failed her at the thought.

"You can be assured he knows," Charlotte said grimly, "although he did not say so in his note."

"What did he say?"

"Only that he had heard from his son and his brother,

Lord Sidney, what charming little parties Oliver and I gave and prayed that he might be permitted the pleasure of attending the one tonight. His messenger brought the note less than an hour ago and was instructed to return with my reply. What could I do but invite him?'' Charlotte gave a mirthless little laugh. "His presence is deemed a triumph for a hostess. If I were not so certain of his reason for coming tonight, I would be honored.''

"Jeremy promised me that he would not tell his father, and he did not say a word about the duke coming here!'' Alyssa cried, her stomach churning. "Even if Carlyle knows, why would he come here?''

Charlotte closed her eyes, her face seeming to grow paler. "Oliver fears he means to humiliate you publicly. Oh, Alyssa, I am so worried. Oliver fears that the duke may hold us responsible for introducing you to Jeremy. You know how important Oliver's political career is to him. Carlyle is a very powerful man, and if he is so disposed, he could end it.''

Alyssa was sick at heart. The Hagars had been such good friends to her, and she could not bear to repay their kindness by unwittingly destroying Oliver's career. "I must talk to the duke privately when he arrives and explain everything to him,'' she said firmly, even though she dreaded the prospect of facing him. "If he has the slightest understanding of his son, he will, I think, be mollified. Please have him brought to me in the green sitting room as soon as he arrives.''

Alyssa squeezed her friend's hand, hurried down the back stairs so she would not be seen by the other guests, and slipped unobserved into the sitting room. She wondered how long she would have to wait for the duke, unaware that he had arrived only a moment after she had gone upstairs to see Charlotte.

Carlyle had been as startled as Alyssa that neither host nor hostess was available to greet their guests. The butler showed him to the drawing room, where early arrivals, including his son, were gathered.

Jeremy's jaw dropped when he saw his father, and he demanded, "What are you doing here?"

"Having heard from both you and Sidney what 'bang-up' parties the Hagars give, I was moved to attend one." Carlyle's eyes swept the room in vain for a vulgar, over-blown female with too much face paint and too little dress, who would be an older copy of the garish Rosina whom he had met in Vauxhall Gardens the previous night. "Where is the divine Alyssa?"

"Upstairs with Mrs. Hagar. She will be so angry at me when she sees you," Jeremy reproached him. "She will think that I broke my word to her that I would not tell you of our betrothal."

"Why should she be angry at you, when her mother informed me of it at Vauxhall last night?"

Relief shone on Jeremy's face. "But, of course," he began as a young officer in the scarlet regimentals of the Hussars, whom he had met during an earlier visit to the Hagars', joined him. Carlyle, who had no desire to converse with other guests while he awaited Miss Raff's arrival, strode into the hall. Unnoticed by the butler who was answering the door, the duke slipped into a little sitting room that he had noticed when he had arrived. He was shocked to find that it was already occupied by the lady of the laburnum.

"Good God!" he exclaimed. "You here!"

Chapter 8

Alyssa's head jerked up in surprise. "Richard!" she cried, her heart giving a happy lurch at seeing the man from the park again. She was seated on a wing chair, her hands clenched tightly together in her lap, trying to shore up her courage before she must face the duke of Carlyle. But all thoughts of that harsh man and the unpleasantness that lay ahead of her were banished by the sight of Richard. She rose to greet him with a radiant smile.

He advanced to her with his singular grace. In his superbly tailored evening garments, he looked even more resplendent than he had in the park. His chocolate-brown frock coat matched his thick curly hair; beige breeches and white silk stockings revealed handsome legs; his snowy white neckcloth was tied with enviable skill, and his waistcoat was also white, but of silk embroidered with green.

Taking her hand in his, he raised it lightly to his lips. The warmth of his lips on her skin, coupled with the light pressure of his hand on hers, sent a shiver of excitement through her.

As he released her hand, he smiled at her in a way that caused her heart to lurch again. Clearly, he was delighted to see her. His gold-flecked eyes were admiring, and his smile was friendly, without the cynicism Alyssa had seen when they had first talked this morning. She found herself wondering what it would be like to be kissed by that sensual mouth.

His soft voice held a hint of laughter as he said, "I trust you managed to reach home this morning without being further molested by runaway toddlers and irate, if incompetent, nursemaids."

She laughed. "Yes, it was quite dull. I collect that you were able to locate Oo-ses's runaway home."

Amusement danced in his eyes. "Yes. He turned out to be Lord Thorn's brat. Why are you hiding yourself in here?"

The answer to that question sent Alyssa's heart plummeting to her toes. The thought of her forthcoming confrontation with the duke of Carlyle was upsetting enough to her, but the possibility that Richard might witness it was intolerable to her. If His Grace created the scene that Charlotte feared he would, Alyssa would appear to be a conniving cradle robber who had entrapped a calfling to further her social and financial ambitions. In what disgust Richard would hold her then. The prospect of his disapproval disturbed her even more than facing the duke, and she suddenly felt exceedingly unwell.

"I . . . I am waiting for someone to come to me," she stammered, wishing that she could flee before Carlyle arrived. At the very least, she had to get Richard out of the room before the duke came to her there.

His face hardened almost imperceptibly about the eyes and mouth. "Are you, now?" His voice, too, had hardened.

She wondered what had caused this change in him, but she was so desperately anxious to be rid of him before the duke descended upon her that she did not have time to refine upon it. "I hope you will not think me rude, but I wish to be private with him."

His hazel eyes glittered like hard gems, their cynicism

72

again firmly in place. "But, of course. I should not like to intrude upon a romantic tête-à-tête. Who is the fortunate gentleman who has won your heart?"

She was so dismayed by his misinterpretation of her words that she said bluntly, "No one has won my heart."

The hard hazel eyes were like yellow diamonds. "I see," he said blandly. "A dalliance. Who is the unfortunate gentleman who has *not* won your heart?"

"You do not under—" She broke off, hearing a noise in the doorway behind her. Her companion glanced toward it. His face suddenly softened, the cynicism magically erased. A look of such pride and love came into his eyes that Alyssa gulped. She wondered if it were his wife who had come to the door, and for the first time in her life envied another woman her husband. She turned, expecting to see an exquisite beauty, and instead saw Jeremy. The way that he looked at Richard caused Alyssa to gulp again as a terrible suspicion suddenly assailed her.

It was confirmed when Jeremy exclaimed happily, "I see you have met Alyssa, Papa. Is she not everything that I said she was?"

Papa! The word echoed and reechoed like the beat of a painfully loud drum in Alyssa's head. Surely this man beside her was too young to be Jeremy's father. Then she remembered that Richard, eighth duke of Carlyle, had been married at sixteen and was only six-and-thirty now. Any remaining doubt Alyssa had was demolished by the mutual affection in the faces of the two men.

The duke exclaimed with profound shock, "She cannot be!"

Seeing the horrified incredulity on his face, her heart again plummeted, not stopping at her toes, but plunging down and down into the vicinity of the Hagars' cellar.

"But of course she is, Papa," Jeremy said cheerfully. He had eyes only for his adored Alyssa, and so did not see, as she did, the anger that seemed to turn his father's

73

eyes to molten fire beneath his fiercely scowling dark brows. "I knew you would be agreeably surprised when you met her."

It was clear to Alyssa that the surprise had been no more agreeable to Carlyle than it had been to her. She cringed as she considered what he must think of her: a woman of an age that branded her as on the shelf using a calfling's first infatuation to tie him to her, even though she was beneath him in station and fortune. She herself would feel the same were she in Carlyle's position and ignorant of her real motive and intention.

The duke turned to the fireplace, struggling to conceal his anger from his son. Watching him, Alyssa realized that Carlyle would never create a humiliating scene, as the Hagars feared, in front of his son. This realization was small comfort to her.

As Jeremy strode across the room to her side, he was oblivious of the sudden tension in the room. "Isn't she divine, Papa?" he asked in such a bewitched tone that had Alyssa not been so distressed, she would have burst out laughing. As it was, she was having considerable difficulty not crying.

Almost as much difficulty as His Grace was having in mastering his rage, but he succeeded so well that when he turned away from the fireplace and faced Jeremy, his countenance was bland, giving no hint of his anger.

"Is she not the most beautiful creature you have ever seen, Papa?" Jeremy persisted.

A smile that did not reach the duke's eyes played on his lips, and he said lightly, "Veracity forces me to confess that I have seen several more beautiful than Miss Raff." Seeing his son stiffen angrily, he added gently, "But before you fly into the boughs, Jeremy, recollect that I have had several more years than you in which to appreciate feminine beauty."

Since Alyssa did not consider herself a beauty, the duke's

74

setdown did not disturb her. What did distress her, however, was his oblique reference to the women whose favors he had enjoyed. She felt as though a knife had been twisted in her heart.

And twisted again when Carlyle gave her a withering look. The softness in his luminous eyes when he had discovered her in the sitting room was gone, she feared forever. Everything had gone wrong tonight. If only she could explain her real intentions to him privately. But with Jeremy here, that was out of the question.

Desperate to escape Carlyle's presence until she could recover her shaken composure, Alyssa put her hand on his son's arm. "Charlotte will think us quite rag-mannered if we absent ourselves from her party any longer. Please escort me back to the drawing room."

The marquess, obliging, led Alyssa from the room. Feeling the duke's penetrating gaze following her, she forced herself to hold her head high and walk at a dignified pace that made her appear even more regal than usual.

When they were in the hall, out of the duke's sight, Alyssa rounded angrily on Jeremy. "Why did you not warn me that your father would be here tonight?"

"I did not know he was coming until I saw him here! But I am glad he came, for it gave you a chance to meet. Contrary to what you feared, he does not oppose our betrothal."

"What?" Alyssa cried in disbelief mixed with alarm. "He cannot have granted his permission for us to wed!"

"He made no objection. It is well that he did not, for I would not have abided by it." Jeremy's chin jutted at a mutinous angle. "Much as it would distress me to go against Papa's wishes, I would do so in this case."

Which the duke no doubt realized. Alyssa had seen how carefully he had concealed his anger from his son. He recognized as clearly as she did the folly of setting Jeremy's obstinate back up. Alyssa wondered what steps such a doting father would take to protect his son from an apparent adventuress like herself. Meanwhile, he was no doubt buying time just as she was. To test this surmise, she inquired innocently, "Has your papa expressed a preference for when we should wed?"

Jeremy ran a finger between his neck and the folds of his cravat as though that garment had become too tight. "Papa prefers that I wait a few months to marry. But that was before he met you. Now that he has done so, I am persuaded that he will give his permission for us to wed soon."

Alyssa thought His Grace would be more likely to renounce both his title and his enormous fortune, but she said hastily, "Even if he gives his permission, do not tease him to wed immediately, for I will not do so for at least a year, and I hold you to your word that our betrothal will remain a secret from everyone else."

"But—" Jeremy began obstinately.

Alyssa cut off his protest. "If you love me at all, Jeremy, you will not want me to be humiliated by people's saying I snatched a cub from his cradle. I could not bear it!" she cried, resorting to theatrics to drive home her point. She clutched her arms over the Empire bodice of her white muslin gown. "I should go into a decline from which I would never recover!"

Much alarmed by this passionate declaration, Jeremy quickly reassured his beloved that he would never do anything to cause her such unhappiness.

Carlyle did not follow Alyssa and his son, but remained behind in the small sitting room. The anger that he had managed with difficulty to conceal from Jeremy was growing hotter by the moment as he came to grips with the unthinkable: that his lovely lady of the laburnum was his son's dreadful Alyssa.

Stoking his temper was the intolerable feeling that he,

as well as his son, had been unforgivably hoaxed by her. He had silently scoffed at Jeremy for permitting himself in his naïveté to be so deceived by a designing female, but he himself had been no less taken in by her. He had been as enchanted as his son. Until she had been revealed to Carlyle as Miss Raff, he had been certain that she was a pattern of propriety: virtuous and highbred. Everything about her from her impeccable manners to her elegant voice and carriage proclaimed her quality. It boggled him that she could be the daughter and sister of those two wretched creatures who had accosted him the previous night at Vauxhall.

He owed his son an apology for thinking him a blind, naive young fool for failing to see at a glance what his love was. Carlyle should have had more faith in Jeremy's intelligence and discernment and less in his own. It both amazed and galled him that he could have been so mistaken about her.

He had sworn a score of years ago that no woman would ever again hoodwink or humiliate him, and none had until Miss Alyssa Raff. She had seemed so delightfully direct, without the flirtatious stratagems her sex so often employed, but, instead, she was a scheming strumpet seeking to ensnare his innocent cub in the parson's mousetrap. Well, damn her, she would not succeed! He would stop her, no matter what. He would not permit her to hurt his son as he had once been hurt. She did not love Jeremy. She had admitted that: *"No one has captured my heart."*

How wretched the heartless jade would make Jeremy if he married her. Beset by an overwhelming urge to destruction as a vent for his fury, the duke looked about the room for a suitable object for sacrifice. Fortunately for Mrs. Hagar and the contents of her sitting room, she displayed considerably more taste in furnishings than she did in her

female friends, and the duke could find no piece sufficiently ugly to merit his smashing of it.

He had no such compunction, however, about what he
would do to Miss Alyssa Raff.

Chapter 9

When Alyssa and Jeremy returned to the drawing room, Jeremy was quickly drawn into a discussion with two other male guests about the most promising horseflesh at the next Newmarket races.

Seeing the Hagars nearby, Alyssa left Jeremy to assure them that she was certain that no matter how angry the duke was, he would not create a scene in front of his son. As she reassured them, they were joined by another couple, and Charlotte hastily changed the subject.

So preoccupied was Alyssa with thoughts of Carlyle that she heard scarcely a word of what was being said. Her head was pounding and her stomach turning queasily as she contemplated what he must think of her. If only she could get him alone again and explain to him what she was about. Glancing nervously about the room, she saw that he had not yet come into the drawing room. Perhaps she could catch him in the hall before he did so and request a private word with him. She was too distressed to wonder why it seemed of such monumental importance that she explain herself to him.

Slipping unnoticed from the drawing room, Alyssa, to her disappointment, found the hall empty. The duke must still be in the small sitting room. She walked resolutely to its door, which was standing open, before her courage could

79

fail her. Carlyle was staring into the unlit fireplace, his back to her.

With trembling knees, she advanced into the room and shut the door behind her. Hearing it, he turned. One look at the hard eyes, glittering with anger, and the equally harsh lines of his face told Alyssa that this would not be a pleasant confrontation.

She forced herself to conceal her anxiety, so intense it bordered on panic, beneath a polite mask and to assume her most regal posture, even though she felt as if her spine had turned to jelly. Her many verbal bouts with her grandfather had taught her the importance of maintaining a cool, dignified composure in the face of her foe, no matter how provoking he was or how frightened she was.

Carlyle said contemptuously, "So now I know your identity, Miss Raff—as in riffraff."

Although much taken aback by his initial slash, she refused to be cowed, saying sweetly, "And you sound like Richard, as in Richard the Third."

"History refuses to serve up to my memory the name of an aging doxy who snatched a rich and titled husband from the cradle," he snapped back.

A small gasp escaped her lips. Even the knowledge that, given the appearance of the situation, his stigmatization of her was justified did not lessen the pain she felt. She plunged ahead in her determination to explain to him that although she had seemingly agreed to wed his son, she had no intention of doing so. "I can understand why you object to your son's marrying at such a young age," she began, "and, believe me, it is not my intention—"

She intended to say "to do so," but he cut her off rudely. "I do not object to his marrying at his age. Naturally, I would prefer him to wait a few years before setting up housekeeping, but I would gladly give my permission for him to wed now if only he chose a suitable bride. My son has a domestic temperament, and I would like him happily settled. I object only to his choice of bride.''

''A suitable choice being one that would bring an excellent dowry and an excellent family connection to the union,'' retorted Alyssa, whose romantic heart was affronted by such cold-blooded alliances. She cared enough about Jeremy to want something better than a loveless marriage for the amiable, good-hearted youth. ''Never mind whether she and Jeremy will suit.''

The thick dark brows snapped together angrily. ''I mind very much! My only thought is for my son's happiness. I care naught for fortune or title so long as I am persuaded that she will make him happy.''

Alyssa, concealing her surprise that the duke cared more for his son's domestic bliss than for the bride's dowry and connection, observed tartly, ''Jeremy thinks that we will be happy.''

Carlyle swept her with a look of such contempt that it seemed to burn the skin from her body. ''You have ensnared him with your wiles. He is a fool not to see you for what you are—a scheming strumpet.''

A gasp escaped Alyssa's lips in her outrage at what he had called her. But the flashing fury in her eyes only made him laugh, as though he were deliberately provoking her into losing her temper.

''So you don't like hearing the truth about yourself,'' he mocked. ''Too bad, I always call a spade a spade—and a strumpet a strumpet.''

No one had ever before questioned either Alyssa's breeding or her virtue, and she was livid. But her long experience in handling her unreasonable grandfather stood her in good stead now. She would not let Carlyle goad her into losing her temper. Choking down her anger, she said with cool hauteur, ''Pray, what do you call yourself, since your own morals are notoriously black?''

His thick brows knit together in a murderous frown, but

when he spoke it was with a coolness that matched her own. "My son's morals, however, are beyond reproach, and he deserves better than you!"

The contempt in his voice stung her into saying, "I should make a magnificent wife."

"Magnificent grief is what you would be to Jeremy!"

She controlled her temper with an iron will, saying tauntingly, "You mean you are not going to wish me happy?"

"I wish you to Jericho. Even if you were a lady of quality and not a trollop from a disgustingly vulgar, low-bred family, your age would be a bar. I know what misery awaits a cub who is wed to a sophisticated woman much older than himself."

Alyssa was so mortified and outraged by his unwarranted insults that her hand longed to slap his arrogant face. She was furious that he could not see at a glance what every other man of her acquaintance had: that she was a woman of propriety and a lady, not a strumpet or even a cyprian. For a moment Alyssa was speechless with humiliation, made all the more painful because for some inexplicable reason she yearned for admiration and respect from this infuriating man, who displayed only insulting contempt for her. With supreme effort, she managed to stop her twitching hand from impacting on his face and contented herself instead with saying coldly, "You know nothing of my family."

"To the contrary, I had the displeasure of meeting your far from charming mother and your equally appalling sister at Vauxhall last night."

Alyssa's cheeks stained a bright red as she remembered with acute embarrassment her distaff relatives' shockingly vulgar dress and appearance as they had departed for Vauxhall. They had looked exactly like what Carlyle had taken them to be. She felt suddenly faint and wondered if her earlier boast to him that she would never need smelling salts had not been premature. In a voice barely above a whisper, she asked, "How did you come to meet them?"

"Your mama accosted me on the mistaken assumption that we were about to become related."

"So that is how you learned of the betrothal," Alyssa murmured weakly. As she considered how the haughty, impeccable duke must have felt when two such vulgar, garishly dressed women descended upon him with their shocking revelation about his son, she could almost feel sorry for him. Alyssa wondered what he had said to her mama. Whatever it was, she was certain that it was responsible for Mrs. Raff's and Rosina's bad humor today. Closing her eyes, she wished that the floor beneath her feet might open up so that she could join her heart, which was still down in the vicinity of the Hagars' cellar. It was a long moment before she could bring herself to open her eyes again. When she did, she saw Carlyle studying her curiously.

"Don't tell me that Fanny—as your brass-faced mama assured me I must call her—did not tell you of our conversation?"

The distaste in his voice angered Alyssa all the more because she knew it was justified. Plucking up her sadly bruised spirit, she managed to answer with freezing bravado, "It must have slipped Mama's mind that she met you."

His bark of sarcastic laughter grated on her ears. "Don't try to hoax me, you little jade. That vulgar creature was preening herself like an overdressed peacock at the honor of being seen conversing with me."

The fact that he was undoubtedly correct added to Alyssa's embarrassment and to her overtaxed temper. "Your consequence is showing, Your Grace!"

"You'll see a great deal more of it, you fortune-hunting harpy, if you do not immediately reject my son's offer."

It crossed Alyssa's mind that Carlyle was attempting to

goad her into behaving like the screaming shrew he thought her to be. Although she would not accommodate him on that score, she was so angry now that any thought of attempting to placate him was gone. How dare he brand her so unjustly without even permitting her to explain her side of the story? Her mind was a chaos of tumultuous and contradictory emotions that left her determined to have retribution from him for his cruel conduct toward her, while somehow simultaneously demonstrating to him how badly he had misjudged both her character and her quality.

Several scenarios on how she might accomplish that flashed through her mind. In one that particularly appealed to her, she would elope to Gretna Green with Jeremy and prove, through her devotion to him, that she was an exemplary wife. But she discarded this scheme, realizing that both she and Jeremy would be the losers in it.

No, the only possible way that she could punish Carlyle was to make him continue to think that she intended to marry his son and that she was even worse than he thought her to be. Nothing else would touch him. Although she had no intention of marrying the marquess, she was no longer willing to confess that to his father, as she had originally intended to do. So long as she maintained the fiction that she would wed Jeremy, she would keep the insulting, overbearing duke squirming like a worm on a fishing hook. Meanwhile, she would secretly make certain that Jeremy developed an aversion to her.

In the end, the haughty, contemptuous duke would see how wrong he had been in his cruel judgment of her. Indeed, she thought bitterly, the only insult that he had not paid her was to offer her money to buy her off from the betrothal, and she observed coldly, "I am surprised, Your Grace, given your aversion to me as a daughter-in-law, that you have not offered me a sum that would make it worth my while to reject your son."

She drew back in surprise, not untouched by fear, at the

dramatic effect her words had on him. It was as if she had touched a flaming torch to dried grass. His eyes blazed with fury; his hands twitched convulsively, and he swore with a fluency and a vocabulary so varied that Alyssa was both amazed and stunned. It took all the pluck that she possessed not to cower and flee before such towering rage.

When finally he curbed his profanity, he said in a voice still seething with anger, "Good God, your mama and sister, who are the boldest trollops I have yet seen, pale in comparison to you!" His furious eyes raked her. "I do not pay extortionists."

To her horror, she realized that he had misinterpreted her words and thought that she was asking to be bought off. She started to correct his mistaken impression, then stopped. The worse he thought her, the more he would rage at the thought that she might succeed in trapping his son into marriage.

Her silence seemed to spur his anger out of control, and he snapped, "Since you are so anxious for money, however, I will offer you another kind of arrangement, a carte blanche with myself."

She stared at him in openmouthed shock, unable to believe her ears. Never before in her life had a man made her a dishonorable offer. To have one come from a man whose regard she had coveted was more than she could bear. A dull red flush spread over her body from the heat of her embarrassment, and she longed to retreat to her bed and cry the night away.

The duke's penetrating eyes reflected surprise and a flash of confusion at her odd reaction, but her pride refused to permit her to confess how much he had wounded her. Exerting an iron self-control, she said in a cold voice, tinged with sarcasm, "I am astonished that you would offer such a poor creature as myself a carte blanche. I fear I am hardly up to your usual exalted standards."

"No, you are not," he said flatly, turning her sarcasm

into a setdown of herself. "But I might possibly find you amusing for a time."

The condescension in his tone set her teeth on edge, and she said tauntingly, "But only think, my lord duke, how it would lower your consequence to be seen with me. All London would be talking."

"No, it would not, because we would not be here," he contradicted bluntly. He gave her a calculating look that chilled her to the bone. "You will enjoy traveling abroad in the first stare of elegance. Would you like to see Venice?"

"I have seen Venice, and I find the romance of the canals there much overrated," she snapped. So he thought her so far beneath him that he would not even be seen in England with her, did he? She would make him pay for his insults to her! Although she was raging, she managed an outward show of calm. "I fear that your generous offer does not tempt me, Your Grace. Having also been to a number of other foreign cities, including Rome, Paris, and Vienna, I prefer London."

His thick dark brows snapped gloweringly together. "Under whose protection were you traveling?"

"Lord Eliot's."

"Good God!" exclaimed the duke, profoundly shocked. "He is old enough to be your grandfather!"

She stared at him in outrage. "He *is*—" She broke off hastily. Let him think the worst of her. It would make him fume all the more until such time as it pleased her to have him learn the truth.

"He *is* what?" Carlyle demanded harshly.

She improvised hastily. "He is a finer man than you will ever be."

He laughed contemptuously. "That irascible old goat! What an exciting lover he must have been. Is that why you have gone from a man with one foot in the grave to a cub with one still in the cradle?"

Her face aflame, she was goaded into retorting, "I infinitely prefer your son to you!"

For an instant, there glittered in his eyes such blazing emotion that it was all she could do to keep from turning and fleeing. "Do you, now?" he jeered.

Without warning, he seized her in his arms and was kissing her with an expertise that proved to her how utterly untrue her previous statement had been.

At first, she fought to free herself, but his arms easily held her helpless in his iron grip. For a slender man, he was exceedingly strong. Then, as the unexpected pleasure of his kiss overwhelmed her, she ceased struggling against what she discovered to her surprise she both liked and wanted very much. As her resistance subsided, he relaxed his hold on her arms, and they crept around him without her realizing what she was doing. Their embrace and kiss became mutual.

When at last he drew away from her, she felt bereft. His kiss had stoked a strange, aching longing within her for she knew not what. So pleasurable was the kiss that she did not even think of protesting his conduct. Alyssa feared that her confusion and inchoate questions were mirrored in her eyes because when he looked into them, he drew his breath in sharply. His own eyes softened and his face was puzzled.

For a moment, there was golden silence between them. Then his face hardened, and he said mockingly, "Better reconsider my offer. You will find me a more skillful lover than my son."

She froze at his careless contempt for her. "As well you should be with all your vast experience at seducing women," she retorted. "But I am persuaded that the skill of a fickle man pales beside the love of a faithful one. Do you think that I would mock Jeremy for his inexperience?"

His eyes widened in surprise. "Of course."

"I would never!"

"God, but you are a superb actress! But not fine enough to hoax me into believing that you care about my son."

"I *do* care about him," she cried, stung. If she had not been so concerned about wounding Jeremy's sensitive young heart and pride, she would have refused his offer, and this humiliating confrontation with his father would never have occurred.

"Liar! You forget that less than an hour ago you admitted to me that no man had captured your heart. What will poor Jeremy think when I tell him that?"

"What would poor Jeremy think if you made his betrothed your mistress?"

"It would open his eyes to what you are!"

"And he will see you for what you are when I tell him you offered me a carte blanche!" she said venomously.

Carlyle started and his face paled, telling Alyssa that she had found the one weapon that could wound him.

"You will not tell Jeremy," he said in a voice that sent a chill along her spine, "or I will make you rue the day you were born. Nor will it do you any good to tell him. I shall deny it and insist that it was you who offered to cry off from your betrothal if I would pay you, which is what you did."

"You misconstrued my words."

"Liar!" he ground out through clenched jaw.

"And what of you?" she demanded coldly. "You would lie to your own son."

"I would do anything, including murder, to keep him from your evil coils."

Alyssa did not doubt that he would, but she was so infuriated by all of the ugly things that he had said of her that she could not resist testing the weapon that he had given her. "So it will be your word against mine," she taunted. "Pray remember, Your Grace, that Jeremy thinks me an angel."

Carlyle looked as though he meant to strangle her on the spot. "And so you are! One of Lucifer's fallen legions!"

"How complimentary you are, Your Grace."

"Let me remind you, Jezebel, that Jeremy cannot marry you without my permission so long as he is a minor. What he feels for you is a silly infatuation that will vanish as quickly as a summer squall. By the time he is of age, he will have long forgotten you."

Alyssa was as certain as Carlyle that he was right, but the smugness of his smile so infuriated her that she cried rashly, "You forget Gretna Green." It occurred to Alyssa that she was playing with fire, but she was too angry to care. "Jeremy's offer of marriage is infinitely more enticing than a temporary carte blanche with you."

His eyes blazed. "Especially when you think the marriage will carry a title and fortune with it, but I promise you, it will bring you neither. If he elopes with you, I shall have your marriage annulled."

"I will make certain that you have no grounds," she retorted, determined to play to the hilt the role he had assigned her. The more convinced he was of her mercenary nature, the more worried he would be until he learned the truth.

"Then I will disinherit him, and he will have nothing."

Knowing how much Carlyle loved his son, she said, "I cannot believe you would do that to him."

His eyes were as hard and cold and cutting as a knife's edge. "I would move heaven and earth to assure that you will never be the next duchess of Carlyle. I promise you that you will gain nothing by marrying him but a life of poverty and grief for him and yourself."

"But Jeremy is your only son," she reminded him. "If you disinherit him, you will have no heir."

He shrugged carelessly. "I am six-and-thirty, young enough to father more sons."

"But that would require you to marry. Can you bear

such a great sacrifice for the sake of an heir?'' Alyssa asked sarcastically.

''I doubt it, but it does not signify. I have several brothers, all of whom are married and blessed with male progeny who can succeed me.''

''Why do you have such an aversion to marriage?''

''I have known too many faithless women like you.'' He raised his eyebrows tauntingly. ''Venice, my dear?''

Goaded beyond rational thought, Alyssa turned and, with head held high, walked to the door. As she threw it open, she snapped back at him, ''No, Gretna Green!''

Chapter 10

Alyssa slammed the door to the sitting room and fled into the Hagars' drawing room. She had scarcely crossed its threshold when Jeremy was at her side, asking, "Where have you been? My word, Alyssa, you look dreadfully out of curl."

"I have the headache." She rubbed her throbbing temples with her slender fingers. "I beg you to take me home at once."

Jeremy immediately ordered his carriage. As he and Alyssa were leaving, the door of the sitting room opened and Carlyle emerged. Alyssa suspected that it had taken him this long to regain control of his temper. Even so, his face was set in hard, forbidding lines. It grew even more forbidding when he saw that they were departing. He said hastily, too hastily, "I am also leaving. Permit me to deliver you in my carriage."

Alyssa suppressed a bitter smile. Clearly he was worried about what she would tell his son of their confrontation. Let him worry! "We must decline your kind offer, Your Grace," she said sweetly. "Jeremy's carriage is already waiting." She gave him a provocative smile. "It has been so *enlightening* to meet you."

If they had been alone, she was certain that her life would have come to an instant end at his hands. But she had checkmated him, and he would spend an uncomfortable hour or two wondering what she was telling his son.

When Alyssa and Jeremy were settled in his carriage, he said reprovingly to Alyssa, "I wish that you had let Papa take us. You had so little time together tonight, and I am persuaded that when you know each other better, you will become fast friends."

Alyssa refrained from saying that she and his papa had had sufficient time together to make them fast enemies. Although she was seething over the duke's insults and dishonorable offer to her, she had no intention of telling his son about them. To do so would sorely wound Jeremy. She could not do that to the boy, even though her pride rebelled at having the insufferable, toplofty duke think that he had cowed her into remaining silent.

But if the duke mistakenly thought his threats had bought her silence, her pride would have to pay that price. It was a trifling compared to the unhappiness she would cause Jeremy and the rift that would occur between him and his father if she broke that silence. Having decided against telling Jeremy about her private session with his father, she must also prevent Carlyle from inadvertently doing so. "Promise me that you will convey to your father immediately upon seeing him my apologies for our early departure, which left me *no chance* to become acquainted with him tonight."

"I will," Jeremy assured her. "I am persuaded, though, that brief as your time was with Papa, he could not help but be quite taken with you."

Taken enough to murder me, Alyssa thought, resting her pounding head on the quilted satin squabs of the carriage. She wondered again what the duke had said to her mother at Vauxhall. Mrs. Raff's odd behavior today convinced Alyssa that Carlyle had succeeded in intimidating her for the first time in her life.

"Isn't he the best of fathers?" Jeremy asked eagerly.

She could honestly agree with the youth on this point, for however ugly and insulting Carlyle may have been to her, his goal had been to save his son from a dreadful mésalliance, and she could not quarrel with that sincere motive. Indeed, had the duke not outraged her by so misreading her own character, she would have been the first to agree with him that she was not a suitable wife for his son. "Yes, he is. How unfortunate that I could not spend more time becoming acquainted with him." She could not resist adding with secret amusement, "I cannot imagine why I should have been stricken with a headache tonight."

For a few moments, only the clatter of hooves and carriage wheels on the cobblestones broke the silence. Alyssa wondered what Carlyle's duchess had been like that he should have such a distaste for marriage.

"You have told me a great deal about your papa, but you never mention your mama," Alyssa noted. "She was a French princess, was she not?"

Jeremy nodded. "Yes, but I do not remember her at all. She died when my sister, Ellen, was born, and I was not quite two. People say how sad it was for Ellen and me to grow up motherless, but it was not at all. Papa was so devoted to us. He was very different from the fathers of my friends, who could not be plagued with their children. He was never stern and remote or patronizing and overbearing and unreasonable like they were."

"How odd that your papa, young as he was when your mama died, never remarried," Alyssa said, anxious to keep Jeremy talking about his father.

"I used to pester him about it, and he always told me that he did not want to inflict a wicked stepmother on Ellen and me."

Alyssa, possessed by a desire, as strong as it was strange, to learn everything that she could about the duke, prompted Jeremy to talk about him. As she listened in fascination, she was struck again by how very different the charming portrait the youth painted of his father was from the picture the world held of the haughty, cold duke. How different, too, from the harsh, insulting man she had faced tonight.

As the carriage drew up in front of Alyssa's house, she said, "Two of my dearest friends have arrived in London, and I wish that you would go with me to call upon them tomorrow."

It was the first time that Alyssa had asked Jeremy to accompany her anywhere, and he said eagerly, "I shall be honored. Who are they?"

"Lady Braden and her daughter, Letty. Perhaps," she added innocently, "you know them. They originally hailed from Berkshire."

"I do. But how is it that you are acquainted with them?"

"I met them while I was visiting at Ormandy Park, which adjoins their new home in Northumberland."

"Why were you there? You never mentioned visiting Northumberland before."

"I was visiting . . . a . . . a *very distant* relative." Indeed, no one could be more distant than her grandfather was to her now.

Carlyle was slumped in a large wing chair in his book room, staring morosely into the glass of brandy in his hand. He had not been foxed since his teens, but tonight he intended to make up for his years of moderation. Damn Alyssa! She was driving him to drink, to dull the pain of knowing that at this very moment she was destroying the trusting relationship that he had spent nineteen years nurturing with his son. He ached to strangle the perfidious witch.

For the first time in his life, he dreaded facing Jeremy and did not know with whom he was angrier, Alyssa or himself. He had never intended to offer her a carte blanche. But his rage when she had asked for money in exchange for crying off from marrying Jeremy, thus proving just how cruel and uncaring and mercenary she was, coupled with the galling knowledge that he had been as enchanted by— and wrong about—her as his son had, betrayed him into giving her a lethal weapon to turn against him. She had recognized it immediately for what it was, and his threats of dire consequences if she used it clearly had not fazed her.

She was a worthy opponent, he conceded grudgingly. He had insulted her viciously with the intent of unmasking her to his son as a vulgar, screeching shrew. Although the flash in her lovely emerald eyes had told him he had succeeded in infuriating her, he had failed to shake her cool composure. Instead, she had turned the tables on him with disastrous results.

Carlyle had never been so shocked as when he learned that she had been old Lord Eliot's convenient. The Eliots were a very old and illustrious family; His Lordship's fortune was large, his intelligence acute, and his histories critically acclaimed. But, besides being old enough to be Alyssa's grandfather, the sanctimonious old goat was a notorious high stickler and pattern card of propriety, who, in addition to his histories, wrote witheringly critical essays on modern behavior that called for a return to high moral standards. The damned hypocrite! While he had fulminated in print about the morals of others, he had been keeping Alyssa as his mistress.

His Grace could not imagine how a young woman of her spirit and that acerbic old man could have dealt together. And the thought of Eliot's wrinkled old hands touching Alyssa made His Grace oddly furious.

Carlyle, hearing the voices of his son and his butler in the hall, gulped down the contents of his brandy glass to fortify himself for the ordeal that lay ahead. So agitated was he that he was unaware that he still held the empty glass in his hand as he went out to greet Jeremy.

Braced for a dreadful scene, full of recriminations, Carlyle was astonished to see his son smiling happily at him. Jeremy said affably, "I am glad you are here, Papa. I am so eager to hear what you think of Alyssa."

Carlyle was dumbfounded. If Alyssa had revealed anything at all of what had passed between them, Jeremy would know very well indeed what his father thought of her.

And Jeremy would be furious, not smiling.

"She made me promise that I would immediately convey to you her apologies for having to depart, when she had *no chance* to become acquainted with you tonight." Jeremy repeated Alyssa's message faithfully, even to the odd stress that she had placed on "no chance."

"Did she, now?" Carlyle said, startled by the message that his son had unconsciously delivered to him. He was certain that his threats had not induced her silence about their confrontation. So what the devil was her game? He regarded Jeremy through narrowed eyes. "Why did you leave so hastily?"

"Alyssa developed a dreadful headache."

The duke could well imagine that she had, after her session with him, but he asked innocently, "What, pray, was responsible for this affliction?"

"She said she could not imagine what had caused it. Oh, Papa, can't you see now why I love her so?"

"Yes, I can see why you are bewitched by her," his father admitted. "Do you mean to plague me now with pleas for permission to marry her immediately?"

"No, Alyssa said that I must not tease you about that."

Because, the duke thought grimly, she knew it would be a waste of time. Did it also mean that she had begun her campaign to get Jeremy to Gretna Green? Carlyle's lips tightened into a thin, hard line. Not a moment was to be wasted in launching his counterattack. Knowing how much his son loved family gatherings at Beauchamp, he forced a smile to his lips, exclaiming with false enthusiasm, "What a great celebration we shall have when the time comes for you to marry. It shall be a grand affair with all our family—your aunts and uncles and cousins—and friends gathered at Beauchamp to fete you and your bride and to share your joy with you! What a happy day that shall be for all of us! I could not bear it if you were to deny me and all the rest of our family who love you that golden day."

"I would never do that!"

"I am relieved. I know what a fatal attraction an elopement holds for young lovers. When one is wildly in love, it seems so romantic and exciting. Unfortunately, it is neither. The reality of being married over a blacksmith's anvil in Gretna Green by a sham minister, with not a single relative or friend to toast you, is a very shabby way to begin a life together with the woman you love. Yes, it is a sordid piece of business and deservedly scandalous in the eyes of the world. There is never any justification for eloping."

"Never, Papa?"

"Never under any circumstances," his father replied firmly. "Indeed, it would break my heart for a son of mine to become involved in such a sordid, scandalous piece of business. When you wed, I want you to be surrounded by your family and friends."

"I do, too, Papa!" Jeremy exclaimed.

The duke raised his empty brandy glass in a mock toast. "To your wedding day, my son." *May it be several years away.* He turned back toward the book room. "I will see you in the morning."

Carlyle shut himself up again in his book room and poured himself more brandy before again sprawling in the wing chair. He had begun his campaign to keep Miss Alyssa Raff from luring Jeremy to Gretna Green, but he did not delude himself that this was only a first and far from decisive skirmish.

She baffled him, and no woman had ever done that before. Why the devil had she not told his son about his offer

97

of a carte blanche? There could have been no surer way to alienate the boy from his father. Carlyle could think of only one answer to this perplexing question. Her silence also ensured his. He was caught in a quid pro quo. She would not tell Jeremy of his dishonorable proposal, but in return, Carlyle could not tell his son that his faithless betrothed had admitted that she did not love him and would cry off her betrothal for a price. The duke's hands curled into tight fists. Yes, she was a very worthy opponent.

And one he could not help reluctantly admiring. She had not even tried to make herself agreeable to him but, instead, had given him as good as she got. It had been many years since the duke had met a lady of either the haut monde or the demimonde from whom he had received more than token resistance to anything he might say or wish.

Beyond doubt, she was the most singular incognita that he had ever met, neither flirtatious nor coy, neither dramatic nor vulgar. Her modest, tasteful garb was not designed to display flatteringly her superb body. If Lord Eliot were responsible for her manners, he had outdone himself. He had not merely rubbed a veneer of quality over her, he had seemingly infused it into her. If Carlyle had not known what she was, had not heard from her own lips how callously she would barter his son's love, he would swear that she was a lady of quality.

It seemed impossible to him that she could have spent a day under the same roof with that dreadful mother and sister of hers. It was as if they had come from different worlds. She recognized that, too, for her cheeks had reddened with embarrassment when he had told her of their accosting him at Vauxhall. Why the devil hadn't her mother told her about their meeting?

Even more surprising had been Alyssa's obvious shock and outrage when he had offered her a carte blanche. But she had recovered quickly, veiling her emotion with sarcasm.

But most puzzling of all had been their kiss. When it had ended, he had seen in her emerald eyes the startled, questioning look of an innocent given her first hint of love's pleasures. Not that that old curmudgeon, Lord Eliot, had likely given her much pleasure.

Carlyle's thick, dark brows knit together in a puzzled frown. Yes, she gave every indication of being a virtuous, sheltered, well-bred young lady instead of a greedy light-skirt who had sold herself to a man old enough to be her grandfather. What a very clever woman she was.

But not clever enough.

Chapter 11

Alyssa confronted her mother as soon as the older woman arose the following day. "Mama, why did you deliberately seek out the duke of Carlyle at Vauxhall and tell him that I was betrothed to his son? You knew I wanted it kept a secret from him."

Mrs. Raff, who was still in a bright red wrapper with a nightcap covering her hair, exploded into a torrent of sputtering, semiarticulate words. Her eyes blazed with mingled anger and fear. The color of her face darkened to that of her wrapper. She concluded her tirade by crying, "You must break off with that vile man's son immediately!"

Knowing how desperately her mother yearned for any connection at all with the nobility or even the gentry, Alyssa could scarcely believe her ears. Clearly whatever Carlyle had told her, it had frightened and intimidated her brass-faced mother more than her daughter would have thought possible. "Even though the vile man is a duke, Mama?"

"I would not care if he were the king!" Mrs. Raff snapped.

"What did he say to you, Mama?"

But no amount of cajoling by Alyssa could induce Mrs. Raff to divulge that, and the daughter was left to speculate. She had never seen her determined, manipulative mother cowed before, and she rather wished that she could have witnessed the scene.

That afternoon, Jeremy accompanied Alyssa to the Bradens'. When Letty appeared, the astonished look on Jeremy's face told Alyssa how amazed he was at the young lady that Letty had become in the two years since he had last seen her.

"Why, you are positively beautiful," he exclaimed with such surprise in his voice that Letty burst out laughing. The two were soon happily recalling their many childhood adventures together.

After that Alyssa saw to it that she and Jeremy called on the Bradens every day on one pretext or another. She was using Letty as a foil to highlight her own suddenly shrewish behavior toward Jeremy.

Whenever Alyssa addressed him, it was in a condescending, overbearing manner, much reminiscent of those odious fathers of whom he had once complained to her. He could say nothing that she did not either contradict, criticize, or correct in a patronizing manner that made him visibly seethe. She detested acting so hatefully toward him, but she was doing it for his sake. Not only would it be much less painful for him to conclude himself that she was not the woman for him, but he would be more cautious the next time he thought himself in love.

Often Alyssa left Letty and Jeremy alone together while she sought out Lady Braden. Since that night at the Hagars', Alyssa had developed an insatiable curiosity about the duke of Carlyle, and she pumped both his son and Lady Braden constantly about him. Alyssa told herself that she did so to "know thine enemy," but deep in her heart she knew this was not the reason.

Jeremy's tales of his father and the boisterous life at Beauchamp were so charming that they made Alyssa wistful. How much fun the boy and his young aunts and uncles

101

had had growing up there. Not at all like her own austere childhood under her grandfather's stern eye.

Although Lady Braden offered a more detached view of Carlyle, Alyssa was surprised at how highly she regarded him.

From Her Ladyship, Alyssa learned that at Jeremy's age Carlyle, having buried his own father and his wife, had been the head of the House of Carstair and steward of vast estates and fortune, with all the heavy responsibilities these entailed. In addition, he had been father to his own two motherless babies, one of them an invalid, and to eight younger brothers and sisters. It had been a daunting burden for one so young, but he had borne it successfully.

Between the duke, who was devoted to all his young charges, and his dear, charming mama, they had created as happy a family circle as Lady Braden had ever been privileged to see. Beauchamp had been a joyful, boisterous place. It was quieter there now. The brothers and sisters were all married, with the exception of Lord Sidney, and had homes and families of their own.

"A special glow must have vanished from Beauchamp when the dowager duchess died a year ago," Lady Braden said. "But neither Jeremy nor Ellen can ask for a more devoted father. Ellen, poor dear, is the sweetest little thing. She was born with a hip deformity that has rendered her a lifelong invalid. For all the duke's notorious reputation, he takes his obligations, especially to his family, very seriously. He was quite wonderful with all of the children. I wish my own husband had been as good. Admirable though Sir John was, he was a stern father, and he never established the rapport with his children that the duke did."

Alyssa remembered how easily and skillfully His Grace had handled the children in the park. To cover her roiling emotions, she said lightly, "Apparently, he is as successful with children as with women."

A troubled frown creased Lady Braden's forehead. "I

have often wondered if His Grace's reputation was not exaggerated. He spends most of his time at Beauchamp, and whatever his activities when he is in London, his conduct at Beauchamp cannot be faulted. Not once has he ever introduced an inamorata or even a flirt there.''

''What was his wife like?''

''I never met her. Unlike her husband, who was always friendly, she thought herself too far above her neighbors to condescend to be introduced to them.'' Lady Braden sighed. ''But what I heard of her I did not like. There was a good deal of gossip about her that I will not repeat because I do not know for a certainty that it was true. I do know, however, that theirs was not a happy marriage.''

Details of a long forgotten conversation between Lord Eliot and two aristocratic French émigrés, who had visited at Ormandy Park after fleeing the Revolution, drifted back to Alyssa. They had been reminiscing about the Bourbons, and the princess had come up. A mistress of romantic conquest, her outrageous behavior had shocked even the licentious French court. Both visitors had been lavish in praise of her vivacity, wit, and charm. She had been Louis XV's favorite grandchild, and he had indulged her every whim, while making no secret of his distaste for the grandson who would one day be Louis XVI. The princess and her cousin, the future king, grew up despising each other. She insulted him and his young wife with her rapier tongue at every opportunity. When Louis XVI came to the throne, he was determined to be rid of her and hit upon a marriage for her with English royalty as a way of accomplishing this.

''But despite her huge dowry,'' one of the émigrés, the Comte de Luc, had said, ''your pious King George, although wishing to accommodate our king in the interests of good relations, had no desire to shackle one of his own sons to such a notoriously immoral woman. He fobbed her off, instead, on his cousin's young son. Poor boy. I understand he was no more than sixteen.''

"Waste no pity on him!" Lord Eliot had snorted. "His morals were no better than hers. He was as flagrantly unfaithful to her as she was to him."

The Comte de Luc had shrugged. "Is it not the way with arranged marriages?"

As the days passed, Jeremy grew so increasingly disenchanted with Alyssa that she was certain it would only be a matter of days instead of weeks until he cried off the betrothal.

The sooner the better. The more she learned about Carlyle and how devoted a father he was, the more forgiving she was of his conduct toward her at the Hagars'. He reminded her of a mother bear protecting her cubs. Knowing how vulgar and obnoxious Mrs. Raff could be, Alyssa shuddered at what must have occurred between them at Vauxhall. That, together with the circumstances of Alyssa's apparent betrothal to his son, made her more sympathetic with his furious reaction even though her pride was still sorely wounded by his insulting assessment of her. With each day her regret grew that she had given in to her temper and allowed herself to appear even lower than she already seemed to him.

Since the Hagars' party, Alyssa had not ridden again in the park for fear that she might meet the duke there. She could not bear to face him again until he knew the truth. Would he forgive her then, or would he continue to despise her for her deception?

Meanwhile, life with her mother was becoming more intolerable. Since Mrs. Raff's meeting with Carlyle, she had been sullen, evil-tempered, and increasingly more hateful toward her elder daughter, making it very clear that she wanted Alyssa gone from her house. But until Lord Eliot relented, Alyssa had nowhere to go. Charlotte or Lady Braden might take her in, but it could be months before her grandfather let her return to Ormandy Park, and she could not impose upon her friends' hospitality for that long. The only answer, Alyssa decided, was to find a position as a governess or a teacher at a girls' seminary. She had been reading the newspaper advertisements carefully the past few days, but no positions had been offered.

Sometimes when Alyssa and Jeremy were visiting Letty and her mother, they would be joined by George Braden.

Poor George was in the depths of despair. His suit for Sarah Turner seemed hopeless. Her uncle had flatly rejected George's offer, saying that he would, under no circumstances, reconsider this decision. Sir Egbert Turner's stubbornness stemmed, of course, from Thomas Stokes's having offered him a handsome recompense for Sarah's hand. If George's poor darling were forced to marry Stokes, whom she despised and feared, she would fall into a deep decline that would be the end of her.

Sarah's uncle had tried to keep George from seeing his beloved, but the Turner family never arose before noon, and the young lovers managed to meet each morning in the park while the rest of the family was still abed. George lived for that stolen hour in the morning, then moped the remainder of the day.

Jeremy's romantic nature was particularly affronted by his friend's situation, and he went so far as to pour out George's sad story to his father at breakfast one morning ten days after the party at the Hagars'.

Carlyle, who was aware both of Stokes's cruel history with wives and Sir Egbert Turner's greed, privately thought that if George Braden had any gumption at all, he would elope with Sarah. It was the only thing to be done in their case. Once they were married, the duke knew that her uncle would be reluctant to try to have the union annulled, thereby calling public attention and disgust to the forced marriage that he had arranged for her. Carlyle, however, kept these sentiments to himself. He dared not mention the fatal word *elopement* to Jeremy in any context, for he wanted to put no ideas in the boy's head.

But he quickly discovered that they were already there when Jeremy, clearly remembering the lecture he had gotten from his father on the subject, asked timidly, "Do you think there might ever be circumstances under which an elopement is permissible?"

"Never!" the duke answered emphatically, perjuring himself in the higher good of preserving his son from Miss Raff's evil coils.

Jeremy looked so unhappy that his father studied him with worried eyes. Carlyle had subtly interrogated his son daily to find out where matters stood between him and Miss Raff, but what the duke gleaned only confused him. If she were enticing the boy to Gretna Green, Jeremy betrayed no indication of it. But, of course, the jade would have cautioned him against betraying their plans to his father. Carlyle was determined to have another talk with Miss Raff.

The following day Jeremy was once again at the Bradens' with Alyssa. The inexplicable change in his beloved's manner toward him both angered and baffled him. Several times he had remonstrated privately with her about how strongly he objected to the overbearing, condescending way that she was treating him, but she professed a total ignorance as to what he could be talking about and chastised him for being a peagoose, adding to his vexation.

At the moment, however, Jeremy was too excited to be out of humor with anyone. That very morning his father had presented him with a spirited bay gelding that he had coveted, and he was expounding upon its virtues in great detail to Letty, who was as fond of horses as he was. So proud was he of his new acquisition that on the way to the Bradens' he had stopped at the stables to show it to Alyssa, but to his acute disappointment, she had professed to be unimpressed.

Now as he told Letty about his acquisition, Alyssa interrupted him in a querulous tone that sounded disconcertingly like her mama's whining voice. "Jeremy, you are quite overstating the poor nag's merits."

Since Jeremy was convinced that it was impossible to overstate them, he understandably bridled and would have launched into a spirited defense, but Alyssa again cut him off, saying, "I am persuaded that his paces, if indeed he has any, will be dreadfully uneven, and his disposition is clearly *cowish*."

"Cowish!" Jeremy ejaculated in disbelief, preparing to do verbal battle.

"Oh, I am sure it cannot be so," Letty interceded. "You must be mistaken, Alyssa, for I know Jeremy's papa, who prides himself on his horses, would never permit a cowish animal in his stables."

"Of course he would not," Jeremy seconded sharply, flashing Letty a grateful look. "And Papa says I have as good an eye for horseflesh as he himself has."

"Of course you do," Letty agreed loyally, and tried to turn the conversation to a less controversial subject. "Is your coat new? I particularly like the color on you."

Alyssa cast a critical eye on the superbly tailored pine-green frock coat and slandered Jeremy's jacket quite as badly as she had his gelding. "Surely you do not think so, Letty, dear. The color is rather dreary, and the tailoring seems quite shabby to me."

"Dreary!" Letty exclaimed.

"Shabby!" Jeremy protested simultaneously, indignation flushing his face to the color of claret. "Why Papa had Weston himself make it for me."

"Oh, and a very beautiful jacket it is," Letty exclaimed, as bewildered as Jeremy by Alyssa's spurious complaint.

"I cannot agree." Alyssa sniffed with such supercilious disapproval that she drew dagger looks from Jeremy. As her young companions stared at her in disbelief, she suddenly stood up. "Please excuse me; I wish to tell Lady Braden something."

When Alyssa left the room, Letty tried to soothe the young marquess's lacerated feelings. "Truly, Jeremy, your jacket is very beautiful. I am certain that your horse must be, too."

Jeremy was mollified. Growing up in such close proximity to Letty, he had been rather inclined to take her for granted. But now he had come to appreciate her sense of humor, which was as lively as Alyssa's, but Letty never turned that humor or an unjustly critical eye upon him as Alyssa was increasingly wont to do. Jeremy was about to invite Letty to ride with him the following day when he remembered that he had already asked Alyssa at his father's request.

Upon presenting Jeremy with the gelding, the duke had said casually, "Now that you have an extra horse, would you like to invite Miss Raff to ride with you in the park tomorrow morning?"

At the time it had seemed like an excellent idea to Jeremy, who had been anxious to show off his new prize to her. But her maligning of the gelding had considerably dampened his enthusiasm for the outing. How unhappy he had become with Alyssa. Her shrewish behavior had killed his love for her, and he was not about to be shackled to such a termagant as she had revealed herself to be. He would have to cry off their betrothal. He gave heartfelt thanks that it was still a secret, so she would not be publicly embarrassed by its termination.

But how on earth was he to tell her? And when? He had two commitments with her on the morrow: the ride in the morning and the theater in the evening with the Hagars. It would be excessively awkward to cry off until after that performance.

Chapter 12

Lord Sidney Carstair, having been in the duke of Carlyle's black books for the past ten days, was uncharacteristically quiet as he and his elder brother cantered in the park the following day. Never had His Grace, usually the most understanding and tolerant of brothers, given Sidney such a trimming, and all because he had innocently introduced Jeremy to the Oliver Hagars' house.

In vain had Lord Sidney tried to explain to the furious duke that he had done so with the sole and laudable intention of cheering up his nephew. After Carlyle had left the boy in London to return to the ailing Ellen at Beauchamp, he had been in a fit of the dismals. The Hagars' home was always lively and amusing. While it was true that one met some unusual people there, they were always entertaining, and none of them, to Lord Sidney's knowledge, had been actually disreputable. So he had been shocked to learn that Miss Raff, who had struck him as a highbred lady and a pattern of propriety was, in fact, a fallen woman who had ensnared his naive nephew. By now, Lord Sidney heartily wished that he had never met Oliver Hagar.

Longing to restore himself to his brother's good graces, Lord Sidney had eagerly acquiesced when Carlyle had requested his help in diverting Jeremy, who was riding with Miss Raff, so that the duke would be left alone with her.

His Lordship, stealing a nervous glance at his brother's scowling face, decided that he had never seen him in such a black temper.

It would have eased Lord Sidney had he known that the duke's humor stemmed not from anger at his hapless brother but at himself for his inexplicable eagerness to see Miss Alyssa Raff again. He had ridden each morning in the park, hoping to meet her. But not once since their meeting at the Hagars' had she been there, and he knew that she was avoiding him.

Each day he had returned disappointed to Grosvenor Square to find his son going off to spend the day with her, and an irrational irritation that was uncomfortably like jealousy had gnawed at him. Not in twenty years had a woman so plagued him.

He told himself it was concern for his son, but he knew that it was more than that. He was intrigued by her. The contradiction between what she appeared to be and what she was confounded him. Her direct gaze and frank tongue made her seem without guile. There had been no artifice in her concern for Eustice when he lay unconscious. Yet she would entrap a naive, sweet-natured boy for whom she cared not the slightest into a disastrous marriage that would be the ruination of him.

Her inherent poise and unconsciously regal bearing proclaimed her a lady of the first consequence. But from her own lips Carlyle had heard her admission that she had been Lord Eliot's convenient. She could have been no more than fifteen, perhaps younger, when she had become Eliot's plaything. Had she been sold against her will by an avaricious parent to a rutting old man whose fancy she had caught when she was little more than a child? If that had been the case, then Carlyle sincerely pitied her, and he clenched his hands unconsciously in longing to wrap them around a certain elderly neck.

* * *

As Alyssa and Jeremy began their ride, she again found several imaginary faults in his handsome new gelding, even though she had seen no finer horse in London, except for Carlyle's big black. After her unwarranted criticism, Jeremy lapsed into angry silence as they cantered through the park.

Despite the tension between them, Alyssa was happy to be riding again, especially on a spirited hack from Carlyle's justly famous stables. She had sorely missed her early morning excursions the past several days, sacrificing them rather than expose herself to the duke's deserved contempt. A contempt that would be heightened by his erroneous conviction that his threats had frightened her into remaining silent about his offer of a carte blanche. She hated to have him think her so pudding-hearted!

Rounding a curve in the meandering path, she and Jeremy came face-to-face with the duke and his youngest brother. Alyssa's heart turned over at the sight of Carlyle, looking so very handsome in his buckskin breeches and a buff riding coat that was every bit as elegant as the russet green one in which he had wrapped the muddied Master Eustice. His face with its remarkable eyes and thick brows had haunted her thoughts for days. Now, seeing it before her, she was both thrilled and unnerved.

"What a surprise meeting you and Miss Raff here," His Grace said to his son. An ironic undertone to his words told Alyssa that it had been no surprise at all. Their meeting was deliberate, but to what purpose?

Lord Sidney immediately exhorted his nephew to show off his new gelding's paces. Jeremy was delighted to oblige, calling back to Alyssa, "Now you shall see how fine they are."

His tone revealed just how aggrieved he still was with her for her slurs on his mount, and amusement tugged at her lips. It would not be above another day or two before he cried off their engagement. Alyssa, having no desire to be left alone with the duke, started to follow Jeremy and Lord Sidney as they galloped away, but she was checked by Carlyle's hand on her mount's reins.

"Stay." The word was a command, not a request. "I wish to talk to you."

Somehow she managed to conceal her tumultuous emotions beneath a cold voice. "But I, Your Grace, do not wish to talk to you. You have said too much to me already."

"Afraid of me, Miss Raff?" he challenged, a strange gleam in his gold-flecked eyes as he guided their mounts into a secluded spot.

"Of course not!" she protested with more haste than accuracy. "But I cannot imagine that we have anything else to say to each other."

"I want to know why you did not tell my son about my offer of a carte blanche? I do not flatter myself that my threats bought your silence."

"No, they did not," Alyssa replied, feeling considerably more kindly toward him for recognizing that fact. "I applaud your perception."

"Thank you. I have a reputation for acuteness—among other things," he said dryly, edging his mount so that he was very close to her. "And now, pray, assuage my curiosity."

His eyes were no longer mocking but deeply penetrating as they studied her face. His nearness had a most alarming effect on her heart, causing it to beat quite erratically. She remembered what it was like to be kissed by that sensual mouth, and she had no stomach for continuing to deceive him. In a day or so Jeremy would end their betrothal. What would be accomplished by continuing to bait his father now?

"I had no wish to destroy Jeremy's regard for you," she said truthfully. "He would have been deeply hurt, and I will not do that to him." She met Carlyle's startled gaze squarely. "You see, I do care very much about Jeremy."

The duke's eyes narrowed speculatively. "If you think by that to gain my permission to marry him, you are dead wrong. You will never have it."

Once again he had misinterpreted her words. It infuriated her that he always insisted upon thinking the worst of her, and she was goaded into crying, "I do not care!"

The thick, dark brows rose skeptically. "Don't you, now?"

"No," she said, bringing her temper once again in check. Thinking of how astounded and relieved he would be when he learned the truth in a few days, she suddenly smiled mischievously. "I predict a very happy ending to our story!"

His face turned thunderous. "Happy for whom?"

"For everyone concerned," Alyssa said mysteriously.

"Surely you do not include me in that group." The gold-flecked eyes glittered dangerously. "A happy ending in your scheming mind can mean only one thing. You are still determined to elope to Gretna Green!"

It would serve him right to let him think that, but Alyssa no longer found any satisfaction in perpetuating the battle between them. His darkly handsome face and his kiss had haunted her since their meeting at the Hagars'. Now, with her heart beating like a pagan drum in his presence, she was forced to acknowledge to herself how much she had come to care for this man who so despised her.

How bitterly she regretted that her outrage and stung pride had kept her from telling him the truth at the Hagars'. Her desire to chasten him by making him think that she would trap his son into a mésalliance had justifiably earned her his hatred, making what had been meant as punishment for him punishment for her instead. Even when he learned the truth, he would no doubt still hate her for having cruelly deceived him.

"Answer me!" he snapped. "Is it still Gretna Green?"

"You may rest easy on that score, Your Grace. I have no intention of eloping with Jeremy," she said, gazing unflinchingly into eyes that, at her answer, became more perplexed than angry.

"So you have come to appreciate that you would gain nothing by your elopement scheme?"

"It never was a scheme of mine. I could not resist letting you think so after you put me so out of temper at the Hagars', I think understandably so, given your provocation."

"So you concede defeat," he said triumphantly. "Do I have your word of honor that you will not attempt to elope to Gretna Green with my son?"

Her green eyes flashed stormily at his assumption that he had bested her. Cocking her head proudly, she observed in frigidly mocking accents, "But, Your Grace, I am quite astonished that you would bother to ask for a strumpet's word of honor. And a scheming strumpet at that!"

"Have I wronged you, Miss Raff?" he asked quietly, no trace of mockery in either his tone or his eyes.

Her heart fluttered like a drumroll at the sudden softness of his eyes. "Yes, you have wronged me!"

He studied her for a long, silent moment, then said in a voice as soft as a caress, "Give me your promise that you will not elope with my son and then let me hear your story. If I have misjudged you, I shall apologize."

"I swear to you that I will not elope with Jeremy," she said, suddenly eager to confess the truth. But she was prevented from doing so by Jeremy and his uncle's riding up.

"Uncle Sidney says my gelding's paces are superb," Jeremy told her triumphantly.

Alyssa, wishing Jeremy, his gelding, and Uncle Sidney all to Jericho for having robbed her of the opportunity of explaining herself to the duke, raised a skeptical eyebrow but said nothing.

She did not need to. Her look had been sufficient to anger Jeremy. "I say, you are the most provoking creature, Alyssa. Come, let us be on our way."

Reluctantly she rode off with him, not trusting herself to look back at Carlyle.

Chapter 13

Alyssa traveled to Drury Lane that night with the Hagars. When Jeremy joined them at the theater, he was accompanied by George Braden, who had come because Sarah Turner would be attending with her aunt, uncle, their two daughters, and Thomas Stokes.

The Hagar party was scarcely seated in its box when George pointed out the Turners' box to Alyssa and Jeremy. Both Sir Egbert and his lady were large, corpulent, and florid-complected. Their two female progeny had inherited these traits and their mama's horse face that placed them at great disadvantage beside the lovely Sarah. She was such a tiny, frail little thing with a frightened look on her beautiful face that reminded Alyssa of a little lost fawn. How cruel to marry such a sweet, young creature scarcely out of the schoolroom to a man who, although he might be very rich, was thirty-five years older than she, and mean in the bargain.

On the other side of Sarah was Thomas Stokes himself, a thin, wiry man, with eyes as cold and emotionless as stones. The centerpiece of his ugly, dissipated face was a bulbous nose almost as wide as the pinched mouth beneath it. He looked a decade older than his two-and-fifty years and was as unloverlike a man as Alyssa had ever seen.

Meek little Sarah would never dare stand up to a tyrant like that.

Alyssa's perusal of Stokes and Sarah was cut short by the appearance in a box across the way of a stunning woman, dressed in a clinging gown of blue watered silk that enhanced her milk-white skin. Her blond hair curled artfully around her lovely face. It was the famous duchess of Berwick, whose charm was even greater than her beauty.

Alyssa was as enchanted as everyone else by her former neighbor from Northumberland. One of Alyssa's bitterest fights with her grandfather had come when he had prohibited her from seeing the duchess anymore because her morals no longer measured up to his righteous standards. But where grandpapa had seen immorality, Alyssa had seen tragedy. The duchess had won the heart of every man in the kingdom save one—her husband's. And Alyssa knew how much the duchess had loved him. Nothing could be worse than to be married to a man one loved and not have that affection returned. But how could Berwick resist his vivacious duchess? Indeed, how could any man?

Her Grace was followed into her box by a man as elegantly garbed as she, in a brown spotted silk coat over a white embroidered silk waistcoat. His chocolate-brown hair was not powdered, and his darkly handsome face was a perfect foil for the duchess's light coloring. A collective gasp rippled through the theater as the audience recognized the duke of Carlyle. The others in their party went unnoticed as all eyes remained fastened on the duchess and her companion.

Alyssa felt as though her heart had just been dealt a stunning blow.

"She must be Carlyle's latest flirt," Charlotte Hagar whispered. "They make a spectacular couple, don't you think?"

"Yes," Alyssa agreed. In fact, a perfect couple. She was seized by a strong urge to burst into tears but was saved by Jeremy's amazed exclamation: "Why, it is Papa with that dazzling creature!" The youth's tone turned disapproving. "And at his age, too!"

Alyssa could not help laughing. "Your papa is hardly ancient."

"But he is *old*! After all, he is *my father*! Imagine having him take up with women now."

Alyssa regarded Jeremy with surprise. Clearly he had never heard the numerous stories about his father's romantic exploits. She remembered what Lady Braden had said about the duke's conduct being above reproach at Beauchamp. With a twinkling eye, Alyssa teased, "Perhaps your papa has decided that you need a wicked stepmama, after all."

"But that lady does not look at all like a stepmother," he protested.

The duchess looked like what she was, a most alluring creature, but Alyssa hid her unhappiness behind levity. "Pray, Jeremy, what does a stepmother look like?"

"Well," he said slowly, "she would be much older, with gray hair and a sterner countenance and steely eyes."

"Would you wish to have such an unappealing creature as your wife?"

"No," Jeremy admitted. "But that is the kind of woman fathers marry."

Alyssa had no opportunity to respond, for the play was beginning. The appearance of the duke and his charming companion destroyed for Alyssa all enjoyment of the performance that followed. When the curtain descended for the intermission, she had very little notion of what had transpired on the stage. Her thoughts were too preoccupied with the inhabitants of a certain box.

When the Hagars, George, and Jeremy left to greet friends, Alyssa remained behind, saying she was feeling unwell. Before the intermission was a minute old, the duchess of Berwick's box was flooded with admirers. But since Carlyle had disappeared from it, it no longer held any interest for Alyssa. She turned her attention instead to the Turner box, where Sarah had been left alone with Stokes, who was making the most of the opportunity. Alyssa's heart went out to the poor girl as she shrank back, trying to escape Stokes's lecherous hands. She averted her face, which was a study in fear and disgust, from him. This clearly angered him, for he suddenly seized her by the hair, jerked her head around so painfully that tears welled up in Sarah's wide blue eyes, and boxed her ear with his other hand.

Alyssa was so shocked and angered that she longed to march over to the box and give Stokes the same treatment that he had just inflicted upon poor Sarah. If he dared to treat her like that in public before they were married, what would he do to her in private once she was his wife?

"What has given you such disgust?" a soft, caressing voice beside Alyssa asked, sending a tremor of excited happiness coursing through her. She looked up at Carlyle. "I . . . I . . . Nothing."

"Surely something inspired such a profound look of revulsion."

Alyssa nodded her head in the direction of the Turner box. "It was the sight of that odious old Thomas Stokes mauling terrified little Sarah Turner. The poor child is scarcely out of the schoolroom, and she is being forced to marry him."

Carlyle turned to scrutinize the box that Alyssa had indicated. Stokes was still holding Sarah tightly by the hair, forcing her to face him. Whatever he was saying to her clearly terrified her. Helpless tears were streaming down her face.

"Beauty and an old beast," the duke observed succinctly. Turning back to Alyssa, he said in a tone as cold and hard as winter ice, "You know what it is like to be mauled by an old man, do you not?"

Alyssa was uncertain that she had heard him correctly. "What are you talking about?"

"Stokes is not nearly as old as Lord Eliot, and you must have been considerably younger than Sarah Turner when you began living under his protection." His eyes and his voice were oddly furious, but Alyssa was so shocked that she did not notice.

"You have suddenly become very pale, Miss Raff. How disagreeable your experience must have been. Is that why you refused my offer?"

"What offer, Papa?" Jeremy asked, stepping into the box.

His father started in surprise, paled, then, recovering, said smoothly, "Good evening, Jeremy. How are you enjoying the performance?"

"What offer, Papa?" his son repeated, refusing to be put off.

There was a moment of tense silence before Alyssa interposed, "He . . . he suggested that I might like to ride in the park with both of you tomorrow, but I declined."

Carlyle flashed her a quick smile of gratitude.

Hastening to divert the youth's attention, Alyssa said, "Jeremy is quite taken with your companion, Your Grace, but he finds your squiring of her quite shocking for one so stricken in years."

Jeremy colored to the roots of his hair.

Carlyle laughed indulgently. "Think I'm making a cake of myself in my dotage, do you, Jeremy?"

The youth's blush deepened to the color of his burgundy coat and he whirled angrily on Alyssa. "You did not have to tell him that! You exasperate me beyond endurance."

120

The duke's eyes widened at his son's outburst, but Alyssa's only response was a beatific smile.

The next act was beginning; the Hagars returned to the box, and the duke took his leave.

After the final curtain, Alyssa departed with the Hagars in their carriage, while Jeremy, accompanied by George Braden, rode away in his own equipage.

The marquess had also witnessed Thomas Stokes's behavior toward Sarah and had been as revolted by it as Alyssa. His kind, chivalrous nature was incensed by such ill treatment of a helpless, frightened girl. As his coach moved away from the theater, its wheels clattering over the cobblestones, Jeremy announced to George, with steel in his voice, "Sarah must be saved from that old pig."

"But what are we to do?" George moaned. "Her uncle is adamant that she must marry Stokes. What is to be done?"

"There is only one thing to be done," Jeremy cried impetuously, quite out of patience with George for wailing when he should be plotting. "You must elope to Gretna Green with her."

In the pale light of the carriage lamp, George's face was shocked. "But I would not know how to go about it," he stammered.

" 'Tis very simple. You hire a coach and the fastest horses you can find, collect Sarah and her maid, and dash for the border," Jeremy replied with great practicality.

"Dash for the border?" George echoed faintly in a tone that indicated he thought that only slightly more difficult than flying to the moon.

"Of course you must keep going at top speed and shall have to hire fresh cattle frequently to keep up your pace," Jeremy continued enthusiastically, "but I am told that the Great North Road abounds with posting houses, so that should pose no difficulty."

"Traveling like that, hiring new horses every few miles, I . . . I couldn't."

"Don't be such a pudding heart!" Jeremy exclaimed, disgusted at his friend's lack of bottom. "Dash it, George, if you are so uneasy, I shall accompany you and handle the details. When you meet Sarah in the park tomorrow, find out the best time for her to escape her uncle's house unnoticed tomorrow night."

His friend's face lit up hopefully, then darkened again. "But I . . . I have no blunt for such a journey."

"I'll take care of that, too," Jeremy reassured him, even though he knew that this would be the most difficult aspect of his scheme. Such a journey, its success imperative upon hiring prime cattle and changing them frequently, might well cost several hundred pounds or more. Especially when one considered that food and a private parlor must be provided for Sarah and her maid. Jeremy had only a small portion of that sum in his pockets at the moment, and it would be two weeks before he would receive the next installment of his allowance.

If only he could take his father into his confidence, but Papa had been so emphatic that elopements were never permissible under any circumstances and that he would never condone or even permit his son to assist in one. In the past few days alone, he had told Jeremy at least a half-dozen times how sordid and scandalous and unnecessary he considered such flights, and how happy he was to know that his son would never participate in such a shabby, ramshackle affair.

So where was Jeremy to get the money? He remembered how unsuccessful his previous application to Mr. Page for an advance on his allowance had been. There would be no help from that quarter. Suddenly a happy idea struck Jeremy. He would go to his father with the same request that he had made to Mr. Page, saying he needed the blunt to buy Alyssa a diamond necklace that he had chosen for her. He had yet to give her a betrothal present, and it was past time he presented her with a token of his love. He winced at speaking to his father of either loving Alyssa or giving her a betrothal present, when he planned to cry off their engagement on the morrow. Although he excessively disliked lying to his father about why he needed the money, he saw no other way to save Sarah from that odious Stokes and unite her with her beloved George.

That worthy, however, was again in danger of being overwhelmed by the difficulties attending his elopement. "It will create such a scandal. The doors of polite society will be shut against poor Sarah. No one will receive her, and that would crush her. She must have a chaperone with her."

"She will have her abigail," Jeremy said.

"She don't have one."

Jeremy was undaunted. "We'll borrow your sister's. Letty will see that the girl goes with us."

"Sarah must have a chaperone, too, to lend respectability," George insisted with a mulish look upon his face.

Although George was normally the most obliging of fellows, when he got that look on his face, Jeremy knew that he would adhere to his demand as stubbornly as Jeremy himself and that it was a waste of breath to argue. "Bring your mother."

George looked as though he had suddenly discovered his friend to be a raving lunatic. "My mother would never condone my eloping! Even if she did, which she won't, she is too old for the trip you describe. No, we must find an older woman, but one who is not too old." He broke into a broad grin. "I know, Alyssa. Surely, she will help us. I know that you can persuade her."

Jeremy suppressed a groan at what George was unknowingly asking of him: First, he would have to inform Alyssa that he no longer wished to marry her; then he would somehow have to persuade his jilted betrothed, who gave every indication of abhorring elopements as much as his father, of aiding and abetting him in one.

He would have to try, of course, for George and Sarah's sake, but the prospect of such a task was enough to keep Jeremy awake all night.

Chapter 14

Carlyle breakfasted alone the following morning. It was his second disappointment of the still-young day, for he was eager to talk to his son. But Jeremy had not returned home until the new day was far advanced, and he did not appear for breakfast.

The duke's first disappointment had come when he had not seen Alyssa during his morning ride. Since she had ceded defeat to him the previous day and promised that she would not elope with Jeremy, Carlyle saw no reason why she should continue to avoid him by abandoning her rides in the park.

The events of the preceding day had left him considerably more charitable toward—and confused about—her. The contradictions that baffled him about her seemed to increase with each exposure to her. The previous day, she had again seemed like the frank, delightful woman he had first taken her to be. Since then, he had thought of little else but her. When he had learned from Jeremy that she would be going to the theater, he had decided to go, too, asking his old friend, the duchess of Berwick, to accompany him. He had hoped to steal unobtrusively a few minutes alone with Alyssa to hear her story, but Jeremy, as he had in the park, had returned too soon. As a result, Carlyle was in Alyssa's debt for sparing his son a second time the truth about his dishonorable offer to her.

Images of her flashed through his mind: tilting her head in proud rejection of his silent invitation as she stood by the laburnum tree; fighting to control her spirited chestnut as it reared and plunged; kneeling in the mud beside little Eustice, scornful of her skirts and all else except the injured child on the ground; watching, face frozen with revulsion, as Stokes tormented poor Sarah Turner. The duke had been as disgusted as Alyssa at that sight. His fingers tightened about his fork as he wondered again what Alyssa had suffered at Lord Eliot's hands.

She haunted Carlyle. Perhaps Jeremy had been right to fear his father might be in his dotage and in danger of making a cake of himself. But over his son's betrothed.

Charitable as he was feeling toward her, however, he was still uneasy about how conciliatory she had been in the park, promising not to elope with Jeremy. Yet she had predicted a happy ending to their story. What possible scheme could she have in mind that would achieve that? Whatever it was, she would have to act quickly, for the duke had detected on the previous day an exasperation in his son's manner toward his betrothed that bespoke of fading affection. Yet she had seemed wholly unconcerned and utterly confident that all would end happily for her. If only the detective that Huge Page had hired would return with his report on her past so that he could show it to his son. So far there had been not a word from the man.

A sudden black suspicion as to what Alyssa's strategy might be assailed the duke—and shook him to his soul. Remembering how easily she had fibbed to Jeremy about his offer to her, he wondered whether she could have been lying, too, when she had promised that she would not elope with Jeremy. Had she been lulling Carlyle into relaxing his guard over his son? The painful possibility that Alyssa's sudden agreeability might be nothing more than a trick cost him his appetite. Frowning, he shoved back his chair and jumped up from the table.

Going into the book room to review his accounts, the duke tried to reassure himself that his dark suspicions of Alyssa Raff were unfair and unjust. Surely she could not be that perfidious.

A half hour later Jeremy stood outside the closed door of the book room and screwed up his courage to face his father. The troubled youth had not slept, dreading this day as he had dreaded no other in his life. He hated having to lie to his father about why he needed money, but it was the only way he could hope to help George and Letty. Knowing how much his father abhorred elopements, Jeremy was certain that he had no hope of obtaining the money if he told him the truth.

Most of all, however, Jeremy dreaded breaking the news to Alyssa that he no longer loved her and was crying off their betrothal. He was certain it would be a dreadful scene, full of tears and recriminations. Alyssa would be shocked and heartbroken. But no more shocked than he had been when he realized that his undying love for her had vanished into the ether. Jeremy recalled with discomforting clarity his impassioned avowals to his father of his eternal love for Alyssa. What a gudgeon his father would think him when he learned that Jeremy's "eternal" love had lasted two weeks. But he had learned a valuable lesson. Never again would he offer for a woman until he had been long and well acquainted with her and was certain of his own heart.

Reluctantly, he opened the door of the book room. "Papa, I must talk to you."

The duke looked up from the papers spread in front of him. "Of course, Jeremy. Come in and tell me what is troubling you." As the youth slid into the room, Carlyle gave him a warm, encouraging smile. "You do not look as though you have slept a wink."

Jeremy, whose honest, guileless nature despised deceit, was beset by a sudden overpowering urge to confess to his father the reasons why he had not been able to sleep. Confess that he no longer wished to marry Alyssa and ask his father's advice on how best to cry off his betrothal to her. Confess, too, that he needed money so that George Braden could elope with Sarah Turner. But to tell the truth would end all hope for George and Sarah. So, instead, Jeremy, his tired eyes evading his father's, said nothing.

"You were out very late after the theater?" the duke said finally.

"I was with George Braden. We had much to discuss."

"Such as?" the duke shot back sharply.

Jeremy reddened, his gaze darting nervously about the book-lined room. "Ah . . . ah . . . nothing that would interest you."

The duke's penetrating eyes narrowed suspiciously at his son's odd reaction. "You would be quite amazed at how broad my interests are."

Jeremy remained silent. The duke sighed and gestured for his son to be seated in a chair across the writing table from his own. "What do you wish to discuss with me?"

Jeremy sank gratefully into the chair, blurting out as he did so, "I must have eight hundred pounds today."

"Must have? My dear boy, whatever for?"

Jeremy twisted uneasily in the chair, his eyes fixed somewhere beyond his father's left ear.

"I . . . I wish to buy Alyssa a betrothal gift, and I have picked out the most beautiful diamond necklace for her," he stammered. Since he knew nothing about the price of diamonds, he was uncertain whether the sum he was requesting was outrageously high or unbelievably low for such a necklace.

His father's dark eyebrows rose. "Has Miss Raff been demanding diamonds of you?"

"Oh, no, Papa!" Jeremy cried, his startled eyes meeting his father's for the first time. "Never once has she asked for jewels of any kind."

The duke looked as though he wanted to ask what Alyssa *had* asked for that cost eight hundred pounds, but he said nothing as his searching eyes continued to regard his son.

Jeremy's gaze dropped to the vicinity of his father's chest, and he stammered, "I-I n-naturally wish to present her with a gift befitting a future duchess."

"Naturally," his father said dryly, a thin, unpleasant smile creasing his mouth. "And so you shall."

"Oh, Papa, thank you!" Jeremy cried joyfully, clearly startled at how easily his father had agreed to his request. "I must have the money this morning."

"But you have no need of money, my dear Jeremy. Perhaps you are not aware that the Carlyle jewels include a justly famous diamond necklace that you may give her. It is worth far more than a paltry eight hundred pounds."

It had never occurred to Jeremy that his father might offer him a piece from the family jewels instead of giving him the blunt he needed. He was so stunned and crestfallen at this unexpected turn that it was a long moment before he managed to stammer, "B-but I do not wish to give her that necklace. I do not like it at all."

"I was not aware that you had ever seen it."

Jeremy flushed and stared down at his lap. "Ah . . . g-grandmama showed it to me once, and it is so . . . so . . . so . . . er . . . trumpery."

"Trumpery! My dear boy, I assure you that your betrothed will not think so. But if that particular necklace offends you, there is a spectacular one, reputed to be one of the most beautiful in the world, that was given to your late mama by Louis the Fifteenth. She was his favorite granddaughter, and it was a gift worthy both of a king and of his affection for her. Any woman would be ecstatic over such a rare and splendid gift."

Jeremy grew even redder, opening and closing his mouth wordlessly several times. What was he to do now? He could not rush about London trying to pawn his mama's necklace to raise money to finance his friend's elopement. Finally he faltered, "Please, Papa, I want to give Alyssa something that I myself have chosen for her."

"I do not mean to disparage your taste, but I can assure you that Miss Raff, or any other woman in her right mind, would prefer one of those I have offered you."

"P-perhaps she would, Papa, but I have my heart quite set on giving her the necklace that I picked out for her," Jeremy said. His tone was firmer than it had yet been, but he still could not meet his father's gaze.

Carlyle shrugged indifferently. "Very well."

Jeremy smiled happily, exclaiming, "I knew you would understand."

"Frankly, Jeremy, I do not. But if you insist that it must be the necklace that you picked out, then we shall drive to the jeweler's and purchase it. Where is the shop located?"

"Oh, no, Papa, you cannot come with me!" the youth cried in dismay.

"Why not?"

Jeremy stared at the books behind his father's head. "Only think how mortifying it would be to me to have my father accompanying me while I buy a gift for my betrothed. It would look as though I were not yet a man able to deal with my own affairs. Please, papa, give me the money and let me go alone," Jeremy pleaded, wondering desperately how he had ever managed to get himself into such a coil. He despised himself for lying to his father, but George was depending on him.

Carlyle studied his son for a long moment. Finally he said, "Very well. I shall tell Hugh Page to have the sum you require ready for you by noon."

Jeremy, breathing a long sigh of relief, tried to thank his father, but the duke cut him off, saying, "I own I am a trifle surprised at your sudden wish to make Miss Raff a gift."

"Why?"

The duke shrugged carelessly. "It appeared to me yesterday that your affections for her had diminished."

Jeremy's startled gaze flew up to meet Carlyle's for only the second time since he had entered the room. How astute his father was, and how the son longed to pour out the truth to him.

The duke regarded him lazily through half-closed lids. "Are you still angry with me for refusing you my permission to marry her immediately?"

"No, Papa. We . . . uh . . . we are in no hurry to wed," Jeremy stammered guiltily, thinking of how he was about to break his betrothal.

"I am relieved to hear that," the duke said, not looking in the least relieved. "I had great faith that I could trust you to abide by my wishes and not involve yourself in anything so sordid and scandalous as an elopement to Gretna Green."

Jeremy flinched at the mention of Gretna Green, which caused Carlyle's mouth to tighten ominously. But the youth failed to notice because he was staring fixedly down at his feet in his continuing effort to avoid his father's eyes.

"It is such a comfort to me, my dear boy, to know that you have proved yourself worthy of my trust."

Jeremy was too unhappy to recognize the irony in his father's tone. "Pray, excuse me, Papa. I have much to do today." Without waiting for his father's permission, he turned and fled from the room.

The expression on Carlyle's face as he watched his son's hasty departure was so forbidding that his butler, entering the door that Jeremy had just exited, took one look and retreated with undignified speed.

It was the first time, to the duke's knowledge, that his son had lied to him. So had the cunning Alyssa lied. But, damn her, her plot would not succeed! He knew just how he would stop their runaway marriage to Gretna Green. Miss Raff was in for the shock of her scheming life. Carlyle jumped up and hurried to the door.

First, he must give Hugh Page his marching orders.

Chapter 15

After leaving his father, a much-shaken Jeremy went to the park where George rendezvoused with Sarah each morning. Here the marquess sustained another shock. Much as she loved George and despised Stokes, timid, proper little Sarah was terrified at the prospect of a mad dash to the border and shocked by its impropriety. She would agree to the journey only if Alyssa, whom Sarah held in considerable awe, would accompany her as chaperone. If Alyssa would not go, neither would Sarah.

"Alyssa will go, I promise you," Jeremy said, although he was far from certain that he could convince her.

It was arranged that Sarah would sneak out of her uncle's house at 9:30 P.M. George would be waiting outside for her, while Jeremy would come with the post chaise.

Leaving the young lovers in the park, Jeremy went directly to Alyssa's. The meetings with both his father and Sarah had gone so much worse than he had expected that he was exceedingly nervous and certain that the interview with Alyssa would be the worst of his life.

To his surprise, however, she took her jilting with amazing calm. In fact, as he stumbled about trying to find words to lessen the blow he was delivering her, *Alyssa* seemed to be comforting *him*.

"Do not be so distressed, Jeremy," she said. "I doubted

that your attachment to me was strong and deep enough to survive. I am happy that you have discovered your own mind before we made an irrevocable mistake." She smiled at him without rancor. "I shall always be very fond of you, Jeremy, and I hope that we can remain friends."

Although Alyssa responded to the ending of her betrothal with remarkable understanding and good humor, she proved less amenable to accompanying an elopement party to Gretna Green.

"What does your father say of your scheme?" she asked.

"He cannot know about it until it is over, or he will find a way to stop it. He is not in the least romantic."

"How will you finance the journey without his help?"

Jeremy's courage failed at confessing the role Alyssa had unknowingly played in securing the money for him. "Have no worry, I have all the blunt that we will need," he hastily assured her. "You *must* come with us. Sarah is too frightened to go without you, and she will be forced to marry that cruel old man. It will be the death of her. Do you want to be responsible for putting her in her grave?"

Jeremy embroidered on this theme a dozen different ways, but his former betrothed remained adamantly opposed to making the journey. He departed in defeat after a final assurance to Alyssa that she was little better than Sarah's murderer.

But Jeremy's despair was short-lived. Within ten minutes of leaving Alyssa, he hit upon a new idea. He would pretend that they were to pick her up after Sarah. Once that young lady was safely inside the post chaise, he would order it out of London at top speed. By the time Sarah, who in Jeremy's opinion was rather slow-topped, grasped what was happening, they would be well on their way.

His next visit was to Hugh Page. Jeremy would have to be careful not to arouse Mr. Page's suspicions, for he was a sharp 'un. But that gentleman handed over the money immediately without a single question. Because Mr. Page

134

knew where the best of everything could be had in London, Jeremy said casually, "A friend of mine who does not have his own equipage wishes to take a young lady and her mother, whom he desires to impress, for a drive in the country. He asked me where to go in London to hire a post chaise and prime cattle to draw it. I was at a loss, but I thought perhaps you might know."

"Only place to go is Marsh's," Mr. Page replied so promptly one would almost have thought he had been expecting the question. "Best in town, and the owner won't swindle your . . . friend."

Jeremy quickly discovered that Hugh Page, as always, was right. Marsh's offered the swiftest of chaises and even swifter cattle to draw them. The proprietor, Mr. Marsh, proved to be a jovial, talkative gentleman who soon had Jeremy confiding both the destination and route of his journey. The youth was very glad that he took Mr. Marsh into his confidence, for it turned out that the proprietor was intimately acquainted with the Great North Road, knowing all the best inns and posting houses and every danger spot between London and Gretna Green.

When Jeremy at last departed, he was silently thanking Mr. Page for having recommended such an excellent fellow.

A half hour later, that excellent fellow was thanking Mr. Page in person for the generous reward he had just received for relaying Jeremy's travel plans. There was, Mr. Page assured Mr. Marsh, even greater largess awaiting him if he would carry out but one more small task when Jeremy collected his post chaise and four that night.

After Jeremy's departure, Alyssa paced the floor of her bedchamber with a tormented conscience. Although she was opposed on principle to anything so ramshackle as a runaway marriage, she was as convinced as Jeremy that the only hope for Sarah and George lay in elopement. Alyssa was equally convinced that if meek, spineless Sarah was forced to marry that evil Stokes, he would mistreat her horribly and her life would be very short indeed. The revolting scene between Stokes and poor Sarah that Alyssa had witnessed the previous night at Drury Lane haunted her so that finally she acknowledged that she could not live with herself unless she did everything possible to help Sarah. If that meant Alyssa would have to accompany the eloping couple to Gretna Green, so be it.

Fortunately Mrs. Raff and Rosina were going to Vauxhall that night, so Alyssa would be able to slip away without them knowing of her departure. She would leave her mama a note that she had gone to nurse Charlotte Hagar, who was ill, and most likely would be there several days. Since Alyssa's nursing skills were in much demand, her mother would not find this strange.

Having made her decision, Alyssa sat down immediately, penned a brief note to Jeremy, and had it sent round by hand to Grosvenor Square.

When Jeremy arrived home late that afternoon, tired and irritable after hours spent in arranging the details of the elopement, the note awaited him. Breaking the wafer and unfolding the sheet, he read:

J:
    Where and when should I await you for the journey?
                                        A.

Jeremy gave silent thanks that Alyssa had changed her mind. Although he would have gone forward with the elopement by duping Sarah, he had been dreading the scene that would precipitate. It would be so much easier if Alyssa accompanied them. He refolded the sheet and ordered that a footman be summoned to deliver a note by hand that he would have ready in a very few minutes.

As he dashed up the stairs two at a time, he did not notice that his father, standing in the shadows of the book room, had been a silent witness to his arrival.

Sitting down at his writing table, Jeremy hastily scribbled a message to Alyssa telling her that he would pick her up at 9:00 P.M. sharp at the opposite end of her block from the Charlie's box. Then he added, "I know it will be a long journey, but do not bring more than a single portmanteau with you. Do not be late for—"

The door opened and his father entered. Jeremy was so startled that he nearly upset the inkpot in his haste to shove both Alyssa's message and his reply under a letter that he had received the previous day from his sister, Ellen, in Bath.

Carlyle, to Jeremy's relief, gave no indication of noticing either his son's jerky movements or his discomfort. Instead, he said placidly, "I have come to see the necklace."

Jeremy, his mind entirely focused on the note he had just hidden, echoed blankly, "The necklace?"

"Your present to Alyssa."

"Oh, that necklace," Jeremy said, his mind whirling desperately in an effort to come up with some plausible excuse for not having it. "I . . . I am afraid that there was a problem with its clasp. It had to be repaired. I will not have it until tomorrow."

"A broken clasp! I am shocked that a reputable jeweler would have overlooked such a thing. Whom are you dealing with?"

Jeremy, who was unacquainted with London jewelers, gulped and said airily, "The place in Bond Street."

"I know of several jewelers in Bond Street, some less reputable than others. What is the name of the firm?"

Beads of sweat appeared on Jeremy's upper lip. "I have a dreadful memory for names. I fear that I cannot recall it."

This sounded ridiculous, even to his own ears, but his father only said, "There is a charming pair of diamond earrings among the Carlyle jewels. I thought if they went well with the necklace, you might add them to your gift. Let me show them to you." The duke rummaged in vain for a moment in the pockets of his coat. "Good God, what have I done with them! Quickly, Jeremy, go into my dressing room and see if I laid them there."

The boy rose to obey his father. When he left the room, Carlyle strode over to the writing table, lifted the letter from Ellen, and looked at the two notes beneath it. There was no surprise in his hard, glittering eyes as he read them, only a peculiar twist to his mouth.

When Jeremy returned, the duke was again standing by the door.

"I could not find them," Jeremy said.

The duke held out his hand palm-up. In it rested a pair of large, tear-shaped diamond earrings. "I only this moment found them in a different pocket. Will they match the necklace?"

Jeremy scarcely glanced at the lovely earrings before saying nervously, "No, no, they would not match at all! But I appreciate your offering them to me."

The duke seemed surprised by his son's response. "It has been my experience that a lover cannot give a lady too many jewels, but the decision is yours." He returned the earrings to his pocket. "I wish you to accompany me on my ride in the park tomorrow, Jeremy."

The marquess blanched, stammering. "I-I forgot to tell you that Winston Bentley invited me to the house party that he is having in Sussex, and I have decided to go. In fact, we leave tonight."

"But my dear boy, I distinctly remember you telling me what dreadful bores you found the Bentleys."

His father's memory was quite accurate, and Jeremy

138

grew even paler. "But so many interesting people have been invited, and Sussex is beautiful at this time of year."

"But if you are going to Sussex tonight, how will you pick up your gift to Miss Raff tomorrow?" his father asked reasonably.

Jeremy's white face turned crimson. "I forgot about that. I . . . I . . . it shall have to wait until I return."

"How unfortunate for Miss Raff," the duke said as he walked to the door, where he paused to say, "Have a pleasant trip to, ah, Sussex."

Jeremy wiped the perspiration from his forehead, grabbed his note to Alyssa from beneath Ellen's letter, and concluded the sentence that he had been writing when his father had come in: "Do not be late, for we must pick up Sarah promptly at nine-thirty. If we do not, we run the risk of her being caught. I dare not wait for you if you are not where you should be."

Chapter 16

Mrs. Raff and Rosina departed shortly after eight that
night for Vauxhall. As soon as the door closed behind them,
Alyssa began hasty preparations for her trip to Gretna
Green. She could not begin to squeeze enough for a journey of the length she was about to undertake into the single
portmanteau that Jeremy said he would permit her. She
considered carefully what she must take and decided upon
two muslin gowns and a riding habit with half boots, the
latter in case their post chaise should break down upon the
road, forcing them to take to horses.

Then she composed a note to her mother, saying that she
had gone to nurse Charlotte, who had been stricken with
an influenza so contagious that the entire Hagar household,
including all the servants, was abed with it. That would
keep Mrs. Raff, who shunned even slightly ill people for
fear she might catch their disease, from going to Charlotte's to inquire about her daughter.

At eight minutes to nine, Alyssa, wishing she had never
heard of Sarah Turner or George Braden, pulled her traveling cloak from the wardrobe and reluctantly put it on. As
she did so, her eye fell upon the case on the floor of the
wardrobe in which she kept her medicinal remedies. Both
Rosina and her mother knew that Alyssa never went to tend
a sick person without carrying that case with her. To leave

it behind might arouse their suspicions about her absence and where she had gone. Despite Jeremy's prohibition of more than one piece of baggage, she would have to take the case with her. Grabbing it up, she concealed both it and the portmanteau beneath her traveling cloak, slipped down the steps, and out into the narrow street.

To her relief, it was empty of pedestrians. She cast a wary glance at the Charlie's box on the corner at the opposite end of the block but saw no sign of movement about it. Its occupant was a fat, lazy man who seldom stirred out of the box and was more often asleep at his post than awake. It was a rare night when his voice was heard calling the hour after 11:00 P.M. Although Alyssa hoped that he would not notice her, she was relieved that he was near enough that should some evil footpad come upon her, she could scream for his help. Not that she could count on his rendering any.

Taking a deep breath to calm her taut nerves, she hurried up the street to the corner at the far end of the block, where she shrank back into the shadows, hoping that no passersby would notice her. Her anxiety was increasing by the minute, and she prayed that Jeremy would not be late.

Far in the distance, Alyssa heard the sound of Big Ben beginning to toll the hour. Suddenly the clock was drowned out by the loud clatter of galloping hooves and carriage wheels on the cobblestones. A black post chaise, heavy curtains drawn across its windows, rushed toward her.

She stepped out of the shadows toward it. The carriage slowed, and its door was flung open. Its lamps had not been lit, and its interior was as black as the bottom of a well. As the vehicle shuddered to a stop, she could see nothing within it but an arm reaching out the door to her.

A voice so muffled that she could hardly make out its words called, ''Hurry, Alyssa.''

A pair of hands grabbed the portmanteau and case from her, tossed them into the carriage, then unceremoniously seized her in a steely grip and yanked her inside. The coach started up again so abruptly that she fell across a pair of muscular thighs. She would have been jolted to the floor had not a strong, ungentle hand been clamped about her waist pinioning her to the lap across which she had fallen. She heard the door slam shut as the chaise picked up speed.

She was so dazed and breathless from her precipitous entrance into the carriage that it was a moment before she began to comprehend that something was dreadfully wrong. Fear prickled along her backbone as she lay sprawled, facedown, across a lap to which she was pinned by a hard hold. "Jeremy?" she quavered, certain that it was not his grip that held her captive, for he would never have handled her so roughly.

The only answer she received was a powerful pair of hands lifting her easily and pushing her into the leather seat, so that she was trapped between the side of the post chaise and her mysterious companion's hard body. The interior of the vehicle was still black as tar. She sensed rather than saw that she and the man beside her were the post chaise's only occupants. Thoroughly frightened, she opened her mouth to scream, but a hand hastily closed over it, trapping the sound in her throat.

Alyssa had never been so terrified in her life. Frantically, she tried to fight her captor, but he was far too strong for her and easily kept her pinned in the corner.

The post chaise, which by now was traveling at a wicked pace, swung recklessly around a corner. The heavy curtains across the window swung apart, and light from the windows of the houses they were whipping past, fell on the face of her abductor.

It was Carlyle.

A strange mixture of relief and excitement coursed through Alyssa as she recognized him, but that gave way to fear as she saw the hard, hating look in his eyes. Clearly he would like nothing better than to strangle her.

Seeing the emotions in her eyes as she recognized him, he lifted his hand from her mouth.

"You," she gasped.

"Yes, me! You evil sorceress!"

His contempt flayed like a whip. She tried to shrink back from him, but she was already wedged tightly against the side of the coach. "Where is Jeremy?" she asked, her voice trembling.

"Preparing for his elopement to Gretna Green."

"Oh, God," she gasped. No doubt Jeremy was even now waiting outside her mother's house for her to appear. His note had warned not to be late or she would jeopardize poor Sarah's escape from her uncle's house. How long would Jeremy wait for Alyssa before he would go on to get Sarah? And would timid Sarah agree to the journey without Alyssa's chaperonage? "You must take me back at once!" she cried desperately. "You are ruining everything!"

"That, my beautiful barque of frailty, is exactly what I intend to do. How happy it makes me that Jeremy's lying, faithless bride won't be waiting for him when he comes for her."

Alyssa gasped as she comprehended how totally the duke had misinterpreted the situation. "You don't understand! I'm—"

"Oh, I understand all too well!" he broke in bitterly. "Let me congratulate you, Miss Raff. I never thought that I would ever again permit myself to be deceived by a conniving petticoat, but you very nearly succeeded. I was fool enough to believe the lies that you so convincingly told me yesterday. 'I swear to you that I will not elope with Jeremy.' " Carlyle's soft voice cruelly mimicked the reassuring sincerity with which she had spoken those words to him. "How you must have laughed at me for being such a flat as to believe that! You evil witch! You planned it all, didn't you? You sought to trick me into relaxing my vigil over Jeremy.''

Alyssa could only stare at him, aghast. His words, so contemptuous of both her and himself, made her feel physically ill. ''No, you—''

''You lying doxy! Not only did you lie to me, but you prevailed upon my son to do so, too.''

Alyssa could not see Carlyle's face clearly in the darkness of the carriage but she could feel his fury in the rigidity of his body on the seat next to her. Had Jeremy told his father this morning that he was crying off his betrothal and Carlyle had thought it a lie?

''Fortunately for Jeremy and unfortunately for you,'' Carlyle continued, ''he lacks your enormous talent as a liar. I saw through his silly tale at once. You will never see Gretna Green with my son.''

''For the love of God, let me explain!'' Alyssa cried.

''Save your breath! I will never believe another word from those beautiful lips of yours! You were right yesterday when you told me that I had wronged you. Indeed, I had! For believing that there was any decency or truth in that lovely, perfidious body of yours.''

Her heart breaking, Alyssa pleaded desperately, ''You have got to listen to me before you ruin everything!''

''I cannot tell you what pleasure it gives me to 'ruin everything.' '' An iron thread in his soft voice sent a shiver down her spine. ''My only regret is that I cannot ruin you as well! Unfortunately, Lord Eliot has robbed me of that pleasure. I shall have to settle for making you sufficiently infamous that no other innocent youth such as Jeremy will ever again fall into your matrimonial coils.''

A strangled cry of dismay and alarm escaped Alyssa's throat as the post chaise slowed, then clanked to a stop. Carlyle said coldly, ''We change coaches here, but it will do you no good to create a scene. The men with this vehicle and my own servants are well paid to ignore any protests you might make. You will succeed only in embarrassing yourself."

Alyssa knew that he was right. It would be futile for her to fight him. And foolish, too, for it would only increase his ire at her. So she contented herself with glaring at him as he stepped out and offered her his hand. She ignored it, descending from the post chaise with as much hauteur as a queen. There was a small gleam of reluctant appreciation in Carlyle's eyes as he watched her.

They were in a small clearing where a second carriage, built for speed and comfort, waited, its four horses pawing at the ground, impatient to be on their way. Its lamps had been lit, and in their pale light she noted the duke's crest upon its door.

Her portmanteau and case of medicinal remedies were transferred from the first vehicle. Without a word she climbed into the second equipage. The interior lamp had been lighted, and she saw that it was far more elegant than the first. The seats were of scarlet velvet, and the sides were lined with silk of the same color. Alyssa sank back wearily against the cushions. Carlyle settled on the seat beside her, the door closed, and they were once again alone together.

"How obedient you have become," he observed. "Not even the smallest outcry."

"As you pointed out to me, it would have done me no good. I see no reason to waste my strength or my voice in futile exercise. I can do naught but accept the unhappy fact that I am your prisoner. Where are you taking me?"

"To Beauchamp." Seeing the shock on Alyssa's face at his answer, he sneered. "You will never be mistress of it, as you thought. But you may be mine until I tire of you."

This statement, delivered with such careless certainty of her character, left Alyssa both mortified and heartsick. Her chin rose unconsciously to a proud, defiant angle. "I will not be your convenient."

"As you wish," he said indifferently. "It is immaterial to me, but you might as well have the enjoyment as well as the notoriety of what the world will believe you are."

She stared at him, horror at her imminent ruin mingled with pain at his hatred for her. "Must you refuse to believe the truth? I swear to you, Your Grace, that Jeremy was not lying this morning when he told you that our betrothal is ended."

The stunned look on Carlyle's face told Alyssa that, whatever else Jeremy might have said to his father this morning, he had not revealed that he was crying off the betrothal.

"That was one lie Jeremy spared me!" the duke exclaimed. "It would have been very awkward for him to tell me that and in the next breath ask, as he did, for eight hundred pounds to purchase you a diamond necklace as a betrothal present."

Alyssa could have cried aloud in vexation. So that was the excuse Jeremy had used to get the money he needed for the trip to the Gretna Green! "He did not want it to buy a present for me. The money is to finance the journey to the border."

"So you admit that you two planned to travel to Gretna Green tonight."

"Yes, I admit it," Alyssa cried. "But we were not going there to be married!"

"What other earthly reason would you have to go there?"

Alyssa remembered how certain Jeremy had been that his father would do everything in his considerable power to stop Sarah's and George's elopement if he learned of it. She looked dubiously at the duke, wondering whether she dared to tell him of it. Would he insist on stopping them, thereby condemning Sarah to a dreadful fate?

Carlyle's eyes, which had been studying her intently, narrowed. "What Banbury tale are you going to tell me now?"

he demanded scornfully, settling back against the squab. "Go ahead. I look forward to your performance."

Alyssa swallowed hard. "Remember Sarah Turner, the girl that Thomas Stokes was mistreating at the theater last night? She and George Braden are wildly in love, and it is they who are eloping. Jeremy and I were only helping them."

The duke roared with laughter. "I congratulate you on coming up with such an imaginative tale on the spur of the moment. You would have made a magnificent actress, Miss Raff."

His scorn ate at Alyssa like lye. "You have to believe me!" she cried. "I swear to you it is the truth."

"Just as you swore yesterday that you would not travel to Gretna Green with my son?" he demanded mockingly. "Tell me, Miss Raff, why you found it necessary to accompany this poor runaway couple."

"To lend respectability. You see—"

His shout of derisive laughter cut short her explanation. "*You* lend respectability, you strumpet," he jeered.

The insult was more than she could bear, and her hand lashed up toward his taunting face. But he was too quick for her. His own fingers closed about her wrist before she could slap him.

"Do not try that again, you hellcat," he ground out, "for the consequences will be exceedingly unpleasant for you." He stared into her eyes for a long moment, continuing to hold her wrist in his punishing grasp.

Alyssa met his furious gaze squarely with eyes as angry as his. There was a strange glint in his eyes when he at last released her wrist. "I will grant you this: You have a remarkably fertile imagination when it comes to lying to me. Will it be equally fertile when you try to explain away why you have been living under my protection?"

"You are determined to ruin me, aren't you?"

"But, my dear Miss Raff, I have told you that is impos-

147

sible, since Lord Eliot has already done so. I can only improve upon his effort. But be assured I shall do so with a vengeance.''

"He was not my lover!" she cried in desperation.

"Was he not?" The look in his hazel eyes made her want to shrivel up on the soft velvet seat and die. "Given that magnificent imagination of yours, my dear Miss Raff, what will you next try to convince me of? That the old goat was in reality your grandfather?"

Her head fell back in despair against the scarlet squab as if her slender neck were no longer able to bear the weight.

"So you actually intended to tell me that whisker," he observed mockingly. "Good God, next you will assure me that the sun rises in the west."

Alyssa could not blame Carlyle for refusing to believe her. If only she had told him the truth that night at the Hagars' instead of letting her anger and wounded pride coerce her into seeking retribution. She had taunted him that she would elope with Jeremy, and now he was convinced that was what she had been doing. By failing to confess the truth in the beginning, she had brought the duke's revenge upon herself. Now he was determined to ruin her, and he would succeed.

Her proud posture drooped as she contemplated the bleak future before her. If her puritanical grandfather learned that she had been under the notorious duke of Carlyle's protection, he would never take her back, and she would have nowhere to go. Never again would she see Ormandy Park. The thought was very nearly her undoing. She had to fight to hold back the tears that threatened to overwhelm her, unaware that her expressive face betrayed her painful emotions to Carlyle.

He had been expecting her to turn into a watering pot in an attempt to soften him and was much surprised by her successful struggle to keep from crying. It softened him toward her more than tears ever would have.

After several minutes of silence broken only by the sound of the carriage hurtling through the night, she asked in a subdued voice, "I beg of you, Your Grace, to restore me to my home. Only consider what Jeremy will think of you when he learns that you have abducted me."

"I am taking a page out of your book, my lying Miss Raff. I have left him a note, saying that you came to me offering to jilt him in exchange for my carte blanche." His voice was taunting. "Being a doting father, anxious to save my son from the clutches of such a harpy, I sacrificed myself and accepted your offer."

"He will never believe you."

"Yes, he will. I will soon be able to present him with proof of your former liaison with Lord Eliot. That will disillusion him as nothing else could."

"You cannot find proof of a liaison that never was!" she cried.

"Spare me your lies," he snapped. He moved on the velvet seat, and his thigh brushed against hers, setting off a quivering within her that made her shrink back into the corner to escape his touch. Feeling her reaction, he laughed and moved closer, deliberately brushing against her again.

"Don't! Please!" she cried.

His lips curled in cynical amusement. "Good God, you are an actress of the first water. One would think you were an innocent."

Alyssa, remembering what Lady Braden had said about his never bringing his women to his country seat, said, "Surely you cannot mean to take me to Beauchamp! What will your daughter think?"

"Ellen will know nothing about you. She will be in Bath, taking the waters with her aunt, for two more weeks. By then you will be gone."

Gone and my life ruined! "What a brief affair you have in mind," she remarked bitterly.

"All of my affairs are brief. I bore easily." Cynical amusement glistened in Carlyle's gold-flecked eyes. "But perhaps you can banish boredom by amusing me with tales from your vivid imagination. You can be a latter-day Scheherazade, entertaining her master with her tongue as well as her body to stave off the end."

"I will entertain you with neither!" she cried, wounded to the core by his insouciance.

He grinned wickedly at her. "Won't you, now?" His hands moved suddenly, locking her face between them, forcing her chin up. His lips closed over hers in a hard kiss. She tried to escape him, but he held her fast and continued his plundering kiss. The harder she tried to struggle against him, the more punishing his kiss and his hold upon her became. Clearly, fighting him would only prolong his embrace. He would settle for nothing less than her surrender. She gave it to him, relaxing against the velvet cushions and parting her lips to accept his kiss. When she stopped resisting him, his kiss softened and his mouth explored hers so provocatively that she was soon quivering with excitement. She was both shocked and thrilled by the strange currents coursing through her, and suddenly she was returning his kiss with a passion she had never known she possessed.

It was he who broke off the kiss, a strange light in his gold-flecked eyes. "No wonder you have so bewitched my poor son," he said hoarsely, flinging himself upon the opposite seat where he silently scrutinized her in the pale light of the carriage lamp.

Alyssa turned her face to the scarlet satin lining of the coach to hide the two large tears that she was powerless to keep from coursing down her cheeks.

Chapter 17

Jeremy was chafing at the inexplicable delay in hitching four horses to a sleek traveling carriage. Mr. Marsh remained genial and unperturbed in the face of Jeremy's irritable and increasingly frequent exhortations to hurry, explaining that a wheel had been found to be loose, and he could not permit any patrons of his establishment to set out on such a long journey in a vehicle that was in anything less than prime condition.

For what must have been the twentieth time in the past thirty minutes, Jeremy pulled his watch from his pocket and consulted it only to find that scarcely sixty seconds had passed since the last time he had examined its face. It was already fifteen past nine, and it would take him at least twenty minutes to drive to Alyssa's, then another twenty-five to drive back to get Sarah and George, which was the most critical part of the whole plan.

They would be waiting for him at nine-thirty, and he dared not delay picking them up because of the very real danger that Sarah's flight might be discovered and a search instituted. Jeremy hastily revised his itinerary. The Turner home was only a few minutes away, and common sense dictated that he go to Sarah's first, even though it meant keeping Alyssa waiting for him for more than an hour. Jeremy deeply regretted that, but it could not be helped.

He hoped that she would not be so poor-spirited as to back out of the scheme when he was so late in appearing for her.

At last the horses were hitched, and Jeremy, somewhat mollified by the quality of the two matched pairs that had been assigned to him, bundled Letty's abigail into the carriage and set off to collect Sarah and George.

By traveling through the streets of London at a speed approaching insanity, Jeremy reached Sarah and George at nine-thirty-three. Crouched in the shadows around the corner from the Turner residence, Sarah was in tears that, once she was inside the carriage, turned into strong hysteria.

Jeremy's nerves and temper were further strained when at five past ten, more than an hour after the appointed time, they reached the corner where Alyssa was to await them and found no sign of her. What they did see, however, was her mother and Rosina climbing the steps of their home, having just stepped down from the hackney that had transported them from Vauxhall Gardens.

"Oh, we are in the suds!" Jeremy exclaimed. "Alyssa must have gone back into the house. Now she will be trapped there until her mother and sister are asleep."

"We cannot wait," George said firmly, the first decision that he had made without Jeremy's help since the elopement plans had begun. Over his beloved's tearful protests, he said forcefully, "We must go on immediately. Already Sarah may have been discovered missing and the alarm gone out."

Jeremy signaled the coachman to drive to their next destination, the posting house on the outskirts of London where the two saddle horses he had bespoken earlier in the day awaited him and George.

Sarah was again in hysteria because she would have to make the journey to Gretna Green without Alyssa's respectable and sustaining company. By now, Jeremy was sorely tempted to throttle his friend's beloved. It would be a long, long trip to Gretna Green.

The elopement party was an hour out of London when an unnerving thought struck Jeremy. What if Alyssa had not gone back into the house before their arrival? What if something dreadful had happened to her during that long hour she would have had to wait for his appearance? The more he thought about it, the more worried he became that all was not right with her.

Elsewhere another journey was reaching its end. After Alyssa had turned her face into the scarlet velvet to hide her tears, she laid her head back on the scarlet squab and feigned sleep rather than meet Carlyle's scowling study. Eventually, as the well-sprung equipage raced through the night, her pretense became reality.

Now as the carriage halted, she stirred and reluctantly opened her eyes. The night, which had been warm when they left London, had grown brisk, and Alyssa saw to her surprise that a fur rug had been tucked around her while she slept to ward off the cold. She glanced at Carlyle on the seat opposite her. She had not thought he would have so much consideration for her comfort.

"We are at Beauchamp," he said as the carriage door opened. Jumping lightly down, he extended his hand to her, and she stared up at a stone building that, even in the darkness, was impressive in its size. Twin stone staircases, illuminated by large lamps, curved around from the ground to a broad doorway, its triangular pediment supported by Doric columns.

As they reached the large door, it was swung open by an unseen hand from within, and they stepped into a large entry hall that was more austere than welcoming in its grandeur. Its walls were decorated with alternating round and square reliefs set between engaged columns of por-phyry. The deep wine of this stone was echoed in the ornamentation of the frieze and in the color surrounding the intricate circular plasterwork in the ceiling. Across the hall from the door rose a broad marble staircase.

"Pedley," Carlyle said to the owner of the unseen hand that had opened the door, "I expressly said in my note that no one was to wait up for me, did I not?"

"Yes, Your Grace," said the butler, a portly man in his fifties with thinning gray hair. The start he gave when he saw Alyssa on the duke's arm was very nearly imperceptible. He was less successful, however, in concealing his contempt. Although it flickered only briefly in his shrewd, observant eyes, it told Alyssa that he was in full agreement with his master's low assessment of her character. Unconsciously, she held herself even more regally in the face of his interested gaze. Let him think what he would; she knew her own worth.

The coachman carried in her single portmanteau and small case, setting them on the polished floor. The butler looked down his proper nose at them, but when he spoke, his voice was tonelessly correct. "Your Grace neglected to inform us that he would be accompanied by a guest. In which chamber do you wish us to put her baggage?"

"Do not concern yourself with it, Pedley," the duke ordered in a voice that prohibited dissent, "and take yourself off to bed."

The butler, knowing better than to question his master when he used that tone, reluctantly did as he was bid, leaving Alyssa and Carlyle alone in the hall.

"If Your Grace will excuse me, I wish to follow Pedley's example and retire," she said coolly, bending to pick up her two bags.

"I will handle them," he said, taking them from her.

"I would think stooping to carry bags would be beneath you," she said coldly, "even though abduction is not."

"I warned you that I would do anything to keep my son

154

from marrying you, and I meant it," he said as they went up the broad marble staircase.

She started to tell him again that his son had not been eloping with her but decided it would be useless.

On the upper floor, he stopped before a closed door, saying, "This is my apartment."

"Where is mine?" she demanded with icy dignity. "Or is your thirst for revenge so great, Your Grace, that you mean to force me into your bed as you forced me into your coach? Will you not content yourself with ruining me in the eyes of the world?"

There was a flash of fire in his golden eyes, but he shrugged carelessly. "It is a matter of supreme indifference to me where you sleep."

He continued down the hall past several more doors before stopping in front of one, opening it, and setting her bags inside. The room was so dark she could see nothing. "Use this chamber if you wish. I'll get a candle from my rooms."

He strode off, returning a minute later with a candlestick.

"Now that you have me here, what do you plan to do with me?" Alyssa asked as she took the flickering taper from him.

"That will depend on the talk I shall have with Jeremy when he comes. I expect that will be tomorrow, although he may sulk for a day or two before he appears."

"He will not be here tomorrow, and not because he is sulking," she said with asperity. "It will be several days before he returns from Gretna Green."

His face hardened angrily in the dancing light of the candle. "So you insist upon maintaining the silly fiction that he will still go there." He turned abruptly and stalked back into his own apartments, shutting the door hard behind him.

Alyssa retreated into the chamber that had been assigned

to her and sank down in desolation upon the bed. She had only herself to blame for her predicament. If only she had told Carlyle the truth in the beginning, instead of encouraging him to think the worst of her. How well she had succeeded! His contempt for her cut her to the soul. *"You were right yesterday when you told me that I had wronged you. Indeed, I had! For believing that there was any decency or truth in that lovely, perfidious body of yours."* Even more painful to Alyssa was the realization that his contempt had been as strong for himself as for her. *"I was fool enough to believe the lies that you so convincingly told me yesterday. How you must have laughed at me for being such a flat. I never thought that I would ever again permit myself to be deceived by a conniving petticoat, but you very nearly succeeded."*

Nothing she could do or say now would shake his conviction that she had been eloping to Gretna Green with his son. *"I will never believe another word from those beautiful lips of yours!"* He would not believe the truth until he heard it from Jeremy. But it would be days before the youth returned from the border.

Meanwhile, she would be a prisoner at Beauchamp, and it would be intolerable if he spent the time ripping at her. Alyssa longed for him to kiss her, not condemn her. Tears flooded her eyes, and despair clawed at her soul as she realized that Carlyle held not only her, but her heart captive.

Suddenly she was determined that no matter how provoking he was to her, she would be a model guest, pleasant, agreeable, entertaining. She would try to make him appreciate, even before Jeremy's arrival, how wrong he was in his assessment of her character. Although she was his prisoner, she would be a charming one.

With this determination firmly fixed, she appeared at breakfast the following morning promptly at the appointed hour.

Chapter 18

Carlyle, who prized punctuality, had entered the breakfast parlor only a moment before Alyssa and looked up in surprise from the sideboard at her prompt entrance. Although she had seemed to accept her abduction with unusual equanimity the previous night, he attributed this to shock and could not suppose that such behavior would last. He was braced for an arsenal of female weapons that he abhorred, including pleas, tears, recriminations, threats, and shrewish tantrums. When she had exhausted these, they would get down to hard bargaining.

But, to his surprise, she employed none of those tactics. Instead, after filling her plate from the sideboard, she sat down at the table across from him and discussed a variety of impersonal subjects, never once mentioning either Jeremy or her own situation. She acted as though nothing was in the least out of the ordinary about her visit to Beauchamp.

And she was, Carlyle had to admit, as delightful a guest, male or female, as he had ever entertained. She offered him none of the insipid chatter that too many women bored him with. Instead she was surprisingly well informed and well read. Her observations were astute and spiced with humor. When she disagreed with him, her arguments were well reasoned and provocative. So engrossed did he become in their conversation that he remained at the table long after he had finished eating.

When at last he arose, he found himself reluctant to abandon her company. Knowing how much she enjoyed riding, he invited her to do so with him, and she readily accepted.

When the duke told the groom to saddle Roan Fire for Alyssa, the servant's eyes popped, and he protested, "Your Grace cannot be serious. M'lady could not possibly—"

"Your Grace is very serious," Carlyle interjected, and the groom went reluctantly off to do his bidding.

"He does not approve of your choice. Do you mean for me to break my neck as a way to be rid of me?" Alyssa teased.

But he answered her seriously. "I would not have ordered a mount that I was not certain that you could handle with ease. Roan Fire is spirited, but you will have no difficulty with him."

Nor did she as she and Carlyle rode over the vast and lovely land that was Beauchamp. Her appreciation of its beauty was so apparent and so clearly sincere that he found himself giving her a more extensive tour than he had planned, even showing her his own favorite spot, a hilltop shaded by a single plane tree that offered a splendid view of the elegant classical facade of Beauchamp's south face, its vast gardens, and the River Kennet, flowing at the foot of the slope on which the house had been built. It was where, in those darkest days of his life, he had brought his then infant son, seeking solace for a broken heart.

"How lovely," Alyssa cried when she saw it. "If I lived here, I would come here all the time."

"I do," he confessed, unaccountably pleased by her appreciation of it.

"How can you bear to live in London, when you are surrounded by so much beauty here?" she asked dreamily.

His head swiveled toward her in surprise, and he saw that her eyes were shining in delight at the vista before her. "I spend most of my time at Beauchamp," he confessed. "But I daresay you would find it exceedingly dull here after the excitement of London." His tone was suddenly harsh. "Or Venice or Paris or Vienna."

Alyssa seemed to radiate dignity. "I do not like cities," she said quietly. "They are interesting to visit for a brief time, I grant you, but I much prefer the country. What I find dullest, Your Grace, is endless parties filled with boring, empty chatter and backbiting that passes for conversation among those who lead empty lives."

She urged Roan Fire forward, leaving a startled Carlyle staring after her.

When they returned to the house after their ride, he found himself even more loath to part from her.

She asked whether she might borrow a book from his library, and he led her into the big corner room. Long windows, sunlight streaming through them, alternated with recessed book shelves on the two outside walls. In the corner where these walls met was the duke's large French writing table of mahogany with bronze mounts. On the inside walls paintings alternated with more recessed shelves, all lined with leather-bound volumes. Comfortable settees and chairs upholstered in turquoise brocade had been grouped about the room.

"What a charming room," Alyssa exclaimed as they entered. "It is so light and airy, with all those windows and the white walls. How much more pleasant than the dark paneling most libraries have."

"You see why I spend so much time here," he said, then startled himself by asking her if she would like to remain in the library to read while he checked over some accounts at his writing table.

For the remainder of that day and the next, Carlyle found Alyssa's presence so enjoyable that he invented excuses to himself and to her so that he could be with her constantly. Never once did she mention Jeremy or the reasons that had led to her stay at Beauchamp, and Carlyle found himself reluctant to bring them up for fear of destroying the pleasant, precarious peace between them. He preferred scintillating companionship to sullen entreaties or shrewish recriminations. Nor did he make any romantic advances to her, even though he increasingly ached to have her. His indulgence in this regard surprised him. Usually that was his only interest in a woman, but Alyssa was different.

As they lingered over dessert two nights after her arrival at Beauchamp, the duke studied her in the candlelight. She was exquisite, with her regal bearing, mischievous eyes, and delightful dimple in the cleft of her chin. Simply dressed in a white muslin gown trimmed about the square neck, waist, and hem with wide emerald-green ribbon that matched her eyes, she wore no jewelry. To his astonishment, he found himself wanting to place around her elegant, unadorned neck the Carlyle emeralds which, magnificent as they were, would pale beside the glory of her eyes.

Two days in her company, which he enjoyed more than that of any woman he had ever known, had left him totally bewildered. He had noted with wry amusement that his servants were as perplexed by her as he was. Her deportment, manners, and conversation bespoke excellent breeding and education. When he had tried to question her about the latter, she had turned his query aside, saying politely, "Let us avoid discussing the personal, Your Grace. It will only have us dagger drawing."

Although she tolerated her situation with the equanimity of an adventuress, she had made no attempt to exploit it. Not once had she threatened or demanded, cajoled or cried.

But why not? Studying her across the table through narrowed eyes, he observed, ''You have accepted your stay here with amazing grace and good humor.''

She shrugged. ''I know that my visit, despite your insistence upon it, is no more welcome to you than it is to me. I see no point of making it even more unpleasant for both of us by indulging in a fit of the sullens or strong hysteria.''

''What infinite good sense you display—occasionally,'' he remarked dryly. ''But why have you abandoned your attempts to persuade me that I was wrong about the nature of your journey to the border?''

''You told me that it would be a waste of my breath,'' she reminded him, ''and I am persuaded it would be. You will not believe the truth until you hear it from Jeremy.''

Carlyle studied Alyssa silently, torn by conflicting emotions: hoping on one hand that Jeremy would not come for days so that he could continue to enjoy her company, but on the other, nursing a growing unease about why he had not come. If she had been eloping with Jeremy, the boy's anger, after reading the note that had been left for him, would focus on her, not on his father. But if she were telling the truth, Jeremy would be furious at him. Trying to shake off his sudden anxiety, the duke asked blandly, ''What will you do after Jeremy comes?''

''Accept your apology for so misjudging me and return to London,'' she replied coolly.

His jaw dropped in surprise. Suddenly he felt bereft at the thought of Beauchamp without her. Good God, he was more bewitched by her than his son had been! ''You need not return to London,'' he said hoarsely. ''My offer of a carte blanche still stands.''

Her emerald eyes flashed angrily, and Carlyle watched in fascination as she struggled to control her temper and her tongue. When she succeeded, she said in freezing accents, "I prefer your apology."

His mouth twisted cynically. "But my carte blanche is more lucrative."

"I would starve in the gutter first!" she cried, her head held at its most regal angle.

"My bed and board will be infinitely more agreeable," he snapped back.

A sudden, loud commotion in the entry hall penetrated into the dining room.

"What the devil is going on out there?" he demanded irritably.

He got his answer a second later when the door burst open, and his sister Hester rushed in. Her worried hazel eyes were so intent on him that she did not notice Alyssa, who was still seated at the table.

"Thank God you came so quickly, Richard," she cried. "I have never been so excessively worried in my life."

"What are you talking about?" he demanded in a low, sharp voice. "And why are you back from Bath so soon?"

"Did you not get my letter that we were returning early?"

"No, I did not."

"But if you did not, why are you here?" Her eyes looked beyond her brother, and for the first time, she noticed Alyssa seated at the table. Her mouth formed a shocked O from which no sound emitted for a moment. Then she said stiffly, "I see."

"I sincerely doubt that you do," Carlyle said dryly. "Where is Ellen?"

"She is being carried in," his sister replied, clearly on the verge of tears. "Oh, Richard, she is desperately ill."

He jumped up from the table in alarm. "Good God, what is wrong with her?"

"I don't know. It came on her so suddenly when we were only a few miles from here. She has a dreadful fever and chills and, I fear, perhaps congestion in her chest. I am terrified."

Carlyle ran from the dining room with his sister at his heels.

Chapter 19

Alyssa followed Carlyle and his sister into a cozy little sitting room that was as warm and inviting as the entry hall was cool and austere. The walls were hung with teal-blue silk between the white wainscoting and the wide, elaborately patterned frieze. Two sofas covered in floral chintz flanked the white mantel of the fireplace.

On one of the sofas reclined a girl so delicate in face and form that she reminded Alyssa of a very fragile, very beautiful porcelain doll with enormous brown eyes and thick dark locks that curled about her face.

As Carlyle strode rapidly toward her, she broke into a smile and held out her arms to him. "Papa," she cried in a voice that was as joyful as it was weak, "I am so happy you are here. I have missed you."

He sank down beside her and hugged her as though he hoped by the strength of his embrace to squeeze the illness from her.

When at last he released her, she pleaded softly in a wispy little voice, "Please do not be angry with Aunt Hester for returning early from Bath. It is my fault, for I wanted to come home so badly. I was lonesome for Beauchamp and for you. I plagued her until she finally agreed. I—" Her speech was interrupted by a hacking cough that shook her frail body.

Carlyle turned to Pedley, standing behind him. "Send for Dr. Belding at once."

"Yes, Your Grace, but I do not know if he is home. He went last week to visit his eldest son in Nottingham and may not have returned yet."

As the butler hurried from the room, the duke swore succinctly under his breath. Seeing Alyssa standing beside the door, he said, "You told me once that you were a tolerably good nurse. Would you look at Ellen?"

His eyes were deeply worried. When Alyssa reached Ellen, she understood why. The girl's large eyes were dull, her face was flushed, her frail body racked by chills, and her breathing raspy. Although it was clear that she had a fever, Alyssa was nevertheless startled when she put her hand gently upon her brow and discovered how burning hot it was.

Ellen studied Alyssa curiously. "Who are you?"

Alyssa felt Carlyle, who was standing very close to her, tense. Forcing a smile to her lips, she said lightly, "My name is Alyssa, and I have come to nurse you. I shall have you feeling much better in a day or two." She gave one of Ellen's thin little hands a reassuring squeeze. "But first we must get you into bed."

The duke bent over his sick daughter, slid his arms beneath her frail body, and lifted her as if she were no heavier than a hummingbird. He carried her from the room and up the broad marble staircase, followed by his sister.

Alyssa paused in the hallway to request from Pedley in a voice clearly accustomed to directing a large and well-ordered household the various items that she would need in the sick room.

The look in the astute butler's eyes told her that he had revised his original opinion of both her breeding and her character. Too bad Carlyle was not as perceptive as his butler.

At the top of the stairs, Alyssa hurried down the hall

until she came to a room with a half-open door. Through it, she saw the duke laying Ellen on the bed. Hovering behind him were Lady Hester and a young woman who apparently was Ellen's abigail. Alyssa hurried on to her own room, where she snatched up her medicine case, then went back to Ellen's bedroom.

It was as lovely and delicate as its occupant. The walls were hung with Chinese silk in pale yellow, with matching drapes at the windows. The same yellow silk had been used to upholster the chairs and a chaise that had been placed in front of a large window.

As Alyssa stepped forward to the bed, with its luxurious hangings of yellow brocade, Carlyle irritably eyed the small case she was carrying. "Why did you waste time fetching your jewel case?"

"The 'jewels' it contains are medicinal." She placed the case on a bedside table that held a tray containing a glass and a pitcher of water. Beside the tray was a small portrait of a young woman with a round face and a protruding lower lip. She was very pretty, but the painter had captured a sullen discontent in her large brown eyes and a self-satisfied twist to her mouth that Alyssa found unattractive.

Ellen was once again racked by an unproductive fit of coughing and Alyssa forgot the portrait. Opening the case, she extracted a small bottle and poured a little of its dark contents into the glass.

"First, I want you to drink this," she told Ellen. "It will relieve your cough."

The girl obediently swallowed the liquid, making a face as she did so, but her coughing quickly stopped.

With an almost imperceptible nod of his head, Carlyle indicated that he wished to speak to Alyssa in the hall. Her answering nod was equally discreet. As she went to the door, he dropped a quick kiss on his daughter's forehead. "I shall return in a minute to sit with you, my pet."

Ellen's wan face broke into a smile. "I should like that very much, Papa."

As he stepped into the hall, his face was etched with worry.

Poor man, Alyssa thought. Both of his children were unwittingly causing him considerable anxiety.

"Ellen is very ill, isn't she?" he demanded.

"Yes, and she will be sicker before she is better," Alyssa replied frankly.

"But will she be better?" he demanded in a voice so full of love and concern that it wrenched Alyssa's heart. "Ellen is very delicate, you know."

"I know," Alyssa said soberly. "I cannot promise her recovery, but before I left Northumberland two months ago, there was an epidemic marked by the sudden onset of a high fever, dreadful chills, and a hacking cough. After a day or two, if the patient was properly cared for, it abated as quickly as it had begun. I believe that is what she is suffering from, but I cannot be certain."

"Thank you for being so frank," he said gratefully.

To distract Ellen from her illness, the duke held her hand and told her funny stories about the odd people who lived in London. Alyssa could tell by the strain in his voice how difficult this effort to be amusing was for him.

A half hour later, Lady Hester came to the sick room with word that Dr. Belding was still at Nottingham and not expected back for another two days. "What shall we do?" she asked anxiously.

"We shall bring Ellen through," Alyssa said with such quiet determination that Lady Hester's eyes took on much the same look of reassessment that Pedley's had earlier.

Alyssa removed two bottles from her case and administered draughts from them to the girl, who soon fell into a restless, feverish sleep.

Carlyle, sitting quietly at his daughter's bedside, said,

"You are exhausted, Alyssa. Go to bed. I will stay with her."

"I cannot leave her!" Alyssa exclaimed, aghast at the thought. "The worst is yet to come. It will be a very long night."

"I will be here."

"So will I," Alyssa said stubbornly.

They both stayed at her bedside. As the long night crept by, the man and the woman were happy for each other's company and comfort in their vigil. From time to time, Alyssa gave Ellen medicine from the small arsenal in her case, but despite all Alyssa's efforts, Ellen's fever mounted. Her companions sponged her burning body and soothed her when she thrashed about in delirous nightmares.

Occasionally, in her delirium, Ellen would cry out for her father. He would stroke her cheek and squeeze her hand, murmuring, "I am here, pet." His touch would soothe her, and she would rest more easily until the nightmares came again to torment her.

Alyssa watched him with a lump in her throat. How good he was when he dropped his shield of cynicism. The past two days at Beauchamp in his company had been the happiest of her life.

In the light of the single candle that had been left burning, Alyssa saw that a thick stubble of beard darkened his lower face. His hair was sadly tousled from his running his fingers through it. His clothes, usually immaculate, were rumpled. His elegant tailcoat of blue superfine and the wide muslin cravat that had been so carefully folded about his neck had been shed long ago. He had rolled up the sleeves of his fine linen shirt and undone its top buttons so that his bronzed chest was visible in the V formed by the white material.

His hazel eyes were so glazed with worry and exhaustion that Alyssa could hardly contain her desire to take him in her arms and comfort him. Whatever else he might be, he

168

was a superb father. How deeply she regretted her wretched impulse to make him suffer by thinking that she meant to trap his son into a loveless marriage. Knowing now how protective he was of his children, she appreciated his rage. How could he have thought anything but the worst of her, especially after having been accosted by her mother and sister at Vauxhall.

Alyssa wondered again what had passed between him and her mama that night. He had clearly frightened Mrs. Raff. Since that night, she had been sullen, brooding, and incapable of speaking the duke's name without murderous venom in her voice. And she was a woman who loved revenge even more than the trumpery paste jewels she bedecked herself in. She hated Carlyle so fiercely that if she somehow were to learn that Alyssa was at Beauchamp instead of with Charlotte Hagar, there would be no end to the mischief she would make. And Alyssa could not bear that. She was hopelessly, irrevocably in love with Carlyle. Above all else she wanted to go quietly back to London and cause him no more trouble than she already had.

Furthermore, if Mrs. Raff learned of Alyssa's whereabouts, she could be counted on to inform Lord Eliot immediately of his granddaughter's scandalous behavior. It would end any possibility that he would accept her back at Ormandy again. Her high stickler of a grandfather would cut her off with the same finality that he had cut her father before her.

A few minutes later, Alyssa's gaze fell on the portrait of the woman on Ellen's bedside table. Jeremy had the same round face, brown eyes, and protruding lower lip. The picture must be of Carlyle's late wife. Alyssa wondered what it would have been like to be loved by such a man, to bear him such cherished children.

"Was that your wife?" she whispered, gesturing at the portrait.

The duke glanced at the portrait with such loathing in

his eyes that her frank, unruly tongue blurted, "Did you ever like her?"

He ran his hands irritably through his tousled hair. "Oh, yes, I loved her once! Fool that I was!"

It was as if all the bitterness in the world had been distilled in those few words. He rose and went to the far end of the room, where he parted a drape and stared out into the darkness beyond.

Only Ellen's feverish call of "Papa" brought him back to the bedside.

"I am here, pet," he reassured her, taking her hand again, his face set in an emotionless mask that seemed to have been carved from stone.

As the night waned, Ellen's fever waxed until she seemed to be burning up.

Finally, not long before dawn, Carlyle asked in despair, "She will die, won't she?"

Alyssa glanced at his anguished face and her heart went out to him, but she would not raise false hopes. "I have successfully brought sicker patients through crises, but none has been as frail as Ellen."

He buried his head in his hands, and Alyssa was certain that he was praying.

Chapter 20

At last, when dawn broke, so did Ellen's fever.

"Thank God," Carlyle murmured, a telltale sheen in his eyes.

Alyssa had never loved anyone or anything as much as she did him in that moment. Placing a gentle hand on his muscular shoulder, she told him softly, "Go to bed. There is nothing more that you can do here. Ellen is out of danger. She will sleep for several hours, which is the best thing for her. I am certain now that it is the same illness that I saw in Northumberland."

"How do you come about your nursing skills?" he asked.

She told him about her nurse. "The people that she treated with her herbs and other homemade remedies seemed to get well quicker and live longer than those whom the doctors bled and leeched. I became fascinated and began to try my hand. In time, people began to seek me out."

"And you responded?"

"Yes. It is very satisfying to help make people well."

The expression in his eyes was so strange and unfathomable that she blurted, "What is the matter? Why do you look at me like that?"

His mouth twisted in a half smile. "You are a most unusual—" He broke off.

"Strumpet," she finished bitterly, certain that was what he was thinking. She turned hastily away from him so that he could not see the agony in her eyes.

Alyssa felt him come up behind her. "That is not what I was going to say," he said quietly, placing his hands gently on her arms. Her heart jumped at his unexpected touch. "You need sleep. You must be burned to the core."

The concern in his voice wrenched at her soul. She dared not look at him, fearing that if she did, she would begin to cry.

His fingers moved up and began to massage the stiff muscles of her neck and shoulders. It felt so good that she never wanted him to stop. But she forced herself to say, in a cracking voice, "Please go. Ellen will want you with her when she awakes. I will stay with her for another hour or two, to make certain all is well. Then I will rest."

He said softly, his hands still working to loosen her tight muscles, "Indeed you shall if I have to carry you to your chamber and tie you to the bed."

She could not help smiling. "Your means would defeat your end, Your Grace. I am persuaded that I would not find such restraint conducive to sleep."

His hands dropped away from her back. "I will tell my sister to relieve you in two hours, earlier if you wish." He touched her arm gently again and, in a voice as soft as velvet, said, "Thank you, Alyssa."

A tremor ran through her. The way that he had said her name made it sound like a lyric poem.

Then he was gone.

No longer able to suppress her tears, Alyssa buried her head in her hands and sobbed silently for what could never be, for her doomed love for him.

When Ellen's eyes opened a half hour later, they were no longer dull with fever. She looked about her eagerly, then frowning, asked plaintively, "Where is Papa?"

"He was up with you all night." Alyssa laid a soothing

hand on the girl's brow, relieved to find it as cool as a spring rain. "It would not do to have him fall ill, too, so I ordered him to bed."

"You ordered Papa? I do not believe that anyone could do so."

"You are quite right," Alyssa agreed with a smile. "I merely persuaded him."

As Alyssa talked, she poured a small amount of liquid from one of the bottles in her case into a glass. Easing Ellen into a sitting position, she handed her the glass, saying, "You must drink this vile stuff. Evil though it tastes, it will help make you well."

Obediently Ellen did as she was bid, making a face as she swallowed. Alyssa took the glass, eased her back down onto the pillows, and squeezed her hand. "Now you must sleep again."

The girl clung to her hand. "I am afraid to. I had such dreadful nightmares."

"That was because you had a fever," Alyssa said soothingly. "It is gone now, and the nightmares will not plague you. But to make certain, I will sit here beside you. In the unlikely event that you do have one, I shall awaken you."

Reassured, Ellen closed her eyes, and almost immediately she drifted off into a sound sleep, her hand still holding Alyssa's.

Sitting by the bedside, Alyssa was haunted by the memory of Carlyle there during the night, holding Ellen's hand and comforting her. How different he was from the haughty, overbearing man she had once supposed him to be.

An hour later Lady Hester appeared, accompanied by Pedley bearing a tray of food.

"I have come to have breakfast with you," Lady Hester told Alyssa as Pedley placed the tray on a table at the opposite end of the room from the bed. "And then you shall go rest."

173

"So much food," Alyssa murmured, looking down at plates heaped with meats, eggs, toast, and a large bowl of assorted fruits.

As the two women sat down at the table, Lady Hester said, "Richard was so distressed about Ellen last night that he forgot to introduce us. I am his sister Hester."

"And I am Alyssa," she replied evasively, reluctant to reveal any more about herself.

But Lady Hester was not to be fobbed off so easily. "Why are you at Beauchamp?" she asked bluntly.

"I am not your brother's mistress, if that is what you are asking," Alyssa replied with equal bluntness.

"So he indicated last night. I should have been surprised if you were, for he brings no women here. Which makes me all the more curious to know why *you* should be here."

"I leave that to your brother to explain. Indeed," Alyssa added wryly, "I should like to hear his answer myself."

Lady Hester regarded Alyssa steadily for a long moment before saying, "Whatever the reason, I am grateful that you were here. I do not know what would have happened to Ellen had you not been. I would never have left Bath with her if I had had the tiniest suspicion that she was out of curl."

"You cannot blame yourself," Alyssa said. "This illness comes on very quickly."

The two women began to eat. After a few bites, Lady Hester asked suddenly, "How do you know my brother?"

"Through Jeremy."

Lady Hester smiled. "Isn't he the dearest, most amiable boy. So like his father was before he married that terrible woman."

"Please tell me about your brother's marriage," Alyssa blurted, desperate to find the key to the enigma that was Carlyle. Seeing the sudden hostility in Lady Hester's face, Alyssa added hastily, "I want so to understand him."

Her Ladyship studied Alyssa's expressive face for a long

moment before she said obliquely, "So that is the way it is, is it?" She looked worriedly toward the bed, then began in a whisper so low that it could not possibly be heard by Ellen, even if she were awake: "King George proposed—I should say demanded—the match, telling my father that it was necessary for secret reasons of state and that to refuse it would be a treasonous betrayal of king and country.

"My poor father was torn between his loyalty to the crown and his concern for his son, who was scarcely sixteen then. Papa did not want him wed so young, especially not to a woman six years his elder. He finally agreed that if, after meeting the princess, Richard wished to marry her, he should. So she was sent here to visit."

Lady Hester's face and voice suddenly hardened. "No one could be more charming on those rare occasions when she cared to be. She was a born coquette who was not satisfied until she had conquered every man she met. Once he had been brought to his knees, however, he immediately bored her. My poor brother was a naive stripling whose knowledge of women was restricted to a few dull country girls. Small wonder that he was dazzled by a scintillating, sophisticated princess raised in a court that prized wit and repartee. He fell wildly in love with her."

Carlyle's bitter words echoed in Alyssa's mind. *"Oh, yes, I loved her once. Fool that I was!"*

"The marriage was performed immediately—before the princess could betray her true deceitful, selfish nature and before we learned of her notorious conduct in France. Once the vows were sealed, however, my brother—indeed, we all to our sorrow—learned the truth. My whole family suffered from her evil mischief and cruel, malicious tongue, but it was my poor brother who bore the brunt of it. She found fault with everything about him." In recounting the story, even all these years later, Lady Hester was still so agitated that her fingers curled unconsciously into angry, unladylike fists.

"At first, they lived here at Beauchamp, which the princess cordially detested. She found life in the country even more boring than motherhood. When Jeremy was born ten months after their wedding, she informed my brother that, having fulfilled her obligation to produce his heir, she would henceforth live in London, where she would do as she wished with whomever she wished. Richard remained here with Jeremy while she conducted herself even more scandalously in London than she had in France.

"It was truly my poor brother's dark night of the soul," his sister said, tears welling up in her eyes at the memory. "He was so unhappy and humiliated that he retreated into a shell that no one but Jeremy could penetrate. He was devoted to the infant."

Alyssa discovered that her own fingers, like Lady Hester's, had unconsciously curled into very unladylike fists. She remembered with painful clarity the duke's words at the Hagars': *"I know what misery awaits a cub who is wed to a sophisticated woman much older than himself."* Alyssa saw Carlyle as he must have been then: three years younger and more naive than Jeremy, but with the same amiable, kindly nature; married to a woman who repaid his adoration by trampling on his love and his tender, adolescent pride, cuckolding him in the bargain. Alyssa's heart ached for him and for the youth he must have been.

"When Jeremy was about fourteen months old, Richard suddenly emerged from his isolation and went to London, where he took up residence with his wife," Lady Hester continued. "Neither of them was seen in public for a month. All visitors were turned away, and none of us ever learned what passed between them. At the end of a month, they each went their own way. My brother, no longer the happy, amiable youth we all loved, but bitter and cynical, launched upon a most dissolute life, gambling and drinking and womanizing.

"Papa, much alarmed, ordered the princess, who was

pregnant with Ellen by then, back to Beauchamp, thinking that if she were here, Richard would return also. But she only laughed at Papa." Lady Hester extracted a white lawn handkerchief from her pocket and dabbed at the tears that had begun trickling down her cheek. "An obstreperous argument erupted between them. During it, Papa suffered a stroke, and although he was still a relatively young man, he died a few days later. She shortened my father's life by many years. Then, on the day of his funeral, she died giving birth to Ellen."

Alyssa swallowed hard. No wonder Carlyle had been so determined to save his son from what he was certain would be a disastrous elopement with a lying, faithless older woman.

"It is said that tragedy can be the making of a man," Lady Hester said thoughtfully. "My brother returned to Beauchamp and shouldered the heavy responsibilities that the two deaths had placed upon him with a maturity far beyond his years. He has rarely gambled or drunk since then. Women, however, are a different story."

She pushed her plate away as though her tale had robbed her of her appetite. "Now, Alyssa, you must get some sleep."

Alyssa nodded, not trusting herself to speak without betraying how deeply she had been affected by the story. At last she understood the enigma, and it only intensified her love for him.

Chapter 21

In London that morning Mrs. Raff donned an elaborate gown of purple-striped silk with a hooped skirt of enormous width and a purple velvet hat trimmed with an ostrich feather. Then she set out for Bond Street to take advantage of Alyssa's absence to pick up a few of the bare necessities of life that her clutch-fisted offspring had denied her: a large bottle of Steele's Lavender Water, a pair of yellow kid gloves, and a huge white satin hat trimmed with such an astonishing array of artificial fruit—strawberries, grapes, tamarinds, and apricots—that it more nearly resembled a fruit bowl than a chapeau. Mrs. Raff was so delighted with it that she could not wait to wear it. She ordered that the more modest purple hat be put in the bandbox in place of her new purchase, which remained upon her head.

It did not occur to Mrs. Raff that her vexing daughter might not have gone where her note had said until the widow chanced to see Charlotte Hagar, looking as if she had never been ill a day in her life, step from Brindley's Bookshop and climb into a curricle waiting in front. Mrs. Raff was some distance from the shop at the time, and her enormous skirt so severely impeded her progress down the crowded street that the vehicle was disappearing around the corner as she reached Brindley's shop.

She stared after the vanished curricle for some moments,

oblivious of the stares of passersby at her new hat, before setting off for the Hagars' house. There, the butler, who was slow-topped under the best of circumstances, was so dumbfounded at being confronted by a woman wearing a satin fruit bowl on her head that he blurted out, ''Miss Raff has not been here in days.''

Her dark suspicions confirmed, Mrs. Raff's next stop was Grosvenor Square, where only moments earlier Jeremy had returned home. He had spent a day and a half on the Great North Road beset by growing fear that something dreadful had happened to Alyssa while she had been left to stand alone on a dark and dangerous street, and that that was why she had not been there when the elopement party belatedly arrived. Although Jeremy was no longer in love with her, he had been responsible for her waiting on the street. If anything had happened to her, it was his fault. By the afternoon of the previous day, his suspicion of foul play had grown into a conviction, and he had announced his intention to return immediately to London while the others continued on to Gretna Green.

He had no hesitancy about leaving George. Once on the road, his friend's initial timidity about the trip had evaporated, and under Jeremy's tutelage, he was soon hiring new teams and ordering ostlers about as though he had been doing so for years. It was clear to Jeremy that his friend could now handle the trip himself without his help, and indeed, it might be better for him if he did. So the young marquess handed George most of his blunt, keeping only a few pounds for himself. Bidding farewell to the runaway couple, Jeremy turned his horse toward London.

He was too exhausted to ride through the night and stopped for a few hours' rest at an inn before riding into London in the morning. His first stop in the city was at Mrs. Raff's, where he was told that Alyssa had left hastily two nights ago to nurse a friend and would be not be back for several days.

Jeremy's worst fears were confirmed: Alyssa was missing. Had been missing for two nights. Swallowing hard, he said, "I must see Mrs. Raff."

"Ain't home," the maid-of-all-work, who had answered the door, replied. "Most likely won't be for hours."

After she shut the door, Jeremy, beside himself with anxiety, stood on the steps, wondering morosely what he should do next. He had no idea how or where to begin searching for Alyssa. As he stared down at the stone steps, he was struck by a sudden, happy inspiration: His father would know what to do. Jeremy had never yet presented his father with a problem that he had been unable to solve.

Heartened, the youth rushed to Grosvenor Square, only to learn to his dismay that his father had unexpectedly gone to Beauchamp on the very night that Jeremy had left for Gretna Green. But His Grace had left a note for his son.

Jeremy broke the wafer and read the brief note, dated three days earlier and written in his father's scrawling hand:

My dear son,

This is the most difficult note that I have written in my life. It is my most unhappy duty to inform you that your divine Alyssa came to me today to reveal your plans to elope tonight to Gretna Green. She had concluded that, given my relative youth, it would likely be a very long time before she could enjoy either the title or the fortune that were her only reasons for wishing to marry you. So she made me an offer: If I would give her a carte blanche (she assures me that I will not be her first protector), she would cry off her engagement to you. If I would not, she would elope with you this very night.

Given her scheming, perfidious nature, I could not let that happen, and I have agreed to her offer. That is why she was not waiting for you when you came for her tonight.

Please understand that, hurtful as this is to you, I do

it only for your sake and your future happiness. I know of no other way to make you see her for what she is in time to save you from a disastrous mistake that will cause you a lifetime of unhappiness.

The paper slipped to the floor from Jeremy's nerveless fingers. He had already learned to his sorrow that Alyssa was a very different woman from what he had first thought her to be, but never had he dreamed that she was the cunning, faithless, mercenary creature his father's note revealed. It was a mark of how far she had fallen in his esteem during the past two weeks that he did not doubt the contents of the note.

She must have gone to his father as soon as Jeremy had cried off their betrothal, lying about the real reason for their journey to Gretna Green. Jeremy's face flushed with anger. What a liar he must appear to be to his father, thanks to Alyssa. He would never have dreamed her capable of such perfidy. He bent down to retrieve the fallen letter from the floor. He must go at once to Beauchamp to expose Alyssa's lies and to try to make amends to his father. Jeremy ordered the fastest cattle in the duke's stables hitched to his chaise immediately.

The order was scarcely out of his mouth when Mrs. Raff rang the bell.

Seeing Jeremy standing in the entry hall, his father's letter dangling from his hand, she pushed boldly past the startled butler, demanding, "Where is my daughter?"

Silently the marquess handed her his father's note. As she finished it, he observed in a sadly disillusioned tone, "I cannot believe it."

"Nor should you," snapped Mrs. Raff. "I know that prim and prissy daughter of mine well enough to know that she would never *accept* a carte blanche from any man, let alone *ask* for one. He has abducted her."

Jeremy had never liked Mrs. Raff, having been shocked

181

and a little horrified by her excessive vulgarity. Now her ridiculous accusation against his father further fueled his temper, already in high heat over Alyssa's treachery, and he cried in a voice quavering with outrage, "My father would never do such a thing!"

"Of course he would!" Mrs. Raff scoffed. "Where is he? Where is my daughter?"

"I don't know where Alyssa is. Papa is at Beauchamp."

Mrs. Raff, playing to the hilt her role of angry mother determined to protect her innocent child, drew herself up indignantly. "I shall go there at once and discover the truth."

"I am leaving now. You may accompany me if you wish," Jeremy offered grudgingly, torn between his strong distaste for her company and an overwhelming desire to see the peal his father would ring over this odious woman for daring to suggest that he would abduct her daughter. Jeremy knew his father to be a man whose conduct was above reproach, and Mrs. Raff would be sorry that she had ever set foot on Beauchamp. So would her daughter when Jeremy had exposed her lie about the nature of the journey to Gretna Green.

Mrs. Raff immediately accepted his invitation, and a few minutes later, the marquess's chaise was awaiting them. Their departure for Beauchamp was somewhat delayed, however, by the difficulty attendant upon getting Mrs. Raff's enormous skirt through the carriage door. With the assistance of two footmen, it was at last bundled into the carriage after much maneuvering that attracted a small knot of interested spectators. It filled the equipage's interior like a giant purple balloon, leaving even the usually amiable Jeremy, who was half buried beneath the billowing silk, fuming at his unwelcome companion.

As the chaise sped through the crowded streets of London, Mrs. Raff was well pleased with the admiring stares the elegant equipage and its prime horses drew from pedestrians. She was even better pleased with the trap in which she now had the high and mighty duke of Carlyle. Since their meeting at Vauxhall, Mrs. Raff had been seething at him. Those hard eyes of his had told her that he would delight in carrying out his Newgate threat. For the first time in her life, a man had truly frightened and cowed her. Even odious Lord Eliot, with his sanctimonious, holier-than-thou attitude had not dared to talk to her with the roughness and contemptuous scorn that Carlyle had. How she had lusted for revenge against him. Yet she had known that she was powerless against him, which had made her all the more furious.

But now he had given her an opportunity for vengeance by abducting Alyssa. It was the only possible way that he could have gotten her to Beauchamp. Although he might think that he could carry off with impunity a Cit's daughter, even the haughty Carlyle would learn that he could not ruin the illustrious Lord Eliot's granddaughter without paying the piper.

Mrs. Raff smiled with glee at what the duke's reaction would be when she revealed to him Alyssa's aristocratic identity. Although Mrs. Raff still feared him, she knew that she now held the trump card over him. She would insist that he marry Alyssa. She knew that he would refuse, and that she would have to go to Lord Eliot. But that rigid old puritan would waste no time in seeing that the duke did right by his granddaughter. Mrs. Raff hoped that she would be privileged to witness the fiery confrontation between those two overbearing, toplofty men whom she so cordially hated.

Yes, indeed, she was very well pleased. How she would enjoy her revenge, and it would have the added advantage of ridding her of her odious elder daughter. Mrs. Raff leaned her head, weighted down from added hairpieces and the bountiful harvest of fruit on her enormous hat, against the quilted squabs of the carriage, a satisfied smirk on her face. How much more impressive to be the present, rather than the future, duke of Carlyle's mother-in-law. Especially, she thought vengefully, when nothing would enrage His Grace more than to be forced to marry her daughter.

Chapter 22

Another unexpected caller chose that day for a surprise visit to Beauchamp. When she arrived late in the afternoon, the duke was at his large mahogany writing table in the library.

He had awakened two hours earlier, much refreshed. His first thought had been of Ellen, his second of Alyssa. He was told both were still asleep. He went into his daughter's room, where she lay in her bed flanked by her abigail on one side and his sister on the other. He laid his hand upon Ellen's cool forehead, then beckoned to Lady Hester to accompany him into the hall.

"There is no need for you to remain here longer. I know how anxious you are to get back to your own family."

His sister nodded. "Yes, I am. Tell Alyssa good-bye for me. I like her." She gave him a penetrating glance. "Why is she here?"

His thick brows knit together in a black scowl. "Ask me no questions about her."

Lady Hester's own eyebrows rose at her brother's abrupt answer. "Very well. If you need me, do not hesitate to send for me."

As Carlyle left his sister, he thought wryly that he himself had almost as many questions about Alyssa as Hester must have. His two days in her company and their long, agonizing night at Ellen's bedside had left him utterly bewildered. No heartless hussy would have shown the care and concern, the tenderness and attentiveness, that Alyssa had for his sick daughter. He was at last willing to believe that she might have been telling him the truth about the flight to Gretna Green. It would also explain why Jeremy had failed to come to Beauchamp.

A disquieting thought gnawed at him: If he had misjudged her character and she had not been lying about the journey to the border, how could he explain her abduction to his son? Carlyle might well have sunk himself beneath reproach in Jeremy's eyes. The duke, increasingly uneasy about the note that he had left for the boy, dispatched a servant posthaste to Grosvenor Square to recover it before Jeremy could read it.

Then Carlyle left word that he wished to see Alyssa immediately upon her awakening. This time, by God, he would have the whole truth from her, including the story of her liaison with Lord Eliot.

But Alyssa slept on, and he went into the library, intending to occupy his mind with business until she awoke. He tried without success to concentrate on the correspondence in front of him on the broad mahogany desk, remembering, instead, Alyssa as she had sat on the brocade settee by the window, reading as he had worked.

There was a scratch at the library door. Carlyle, thinking that at last Alyssa had awakened, called eagerly, "Come in."

But it was Pedley announcing that the duchess of Berwick had paid a surprise visit and was awaiting him in the drawing room.

"Of all the wretched times for Selena to come," Carlyle exclaimed in vexation. Ordinarily he was always happy to see the duchess, who was one of the very few women that he liked, but now he wished her to Jericho. "I have never known her to call without sending word of her intention to do so in advance."

"She bade me to ask your forgiveness for arriving without warning like this, but she spent last night with Lord and Lady Bowdin on her way to Berwick Castle and wishes to see you before she leaves the neighborhood."

The Bowdins' country property, Millbrook, was not far from Beauchamp. Selena had told Carlyle on the night that he had escorted her to the theater that she would soon be stopping there on her way to her husband's country seat. He had told her then that he would still be in London. How had she learned that he was at Beauchamp, after all?

"I suppose I must see her," he said, curious as to what had prompted her surprise visit. "Tell her that I'll join her shortly."

When he emerged from the library into the entry hall, Alyssa was coming down the marble staircase. Damnation, he thought as he watched her regal descent, why could she not have awakened ten minutes earlier? He wanted so to talk to her, but now he would have to see the duchess first.

"I am told that you wished to see me immediately, Your Grace," Alyssa said politely.

"Yes, I do, but I have an unexpected visitor that I must see first. Wait for me in the library. I'll be with you as quickly as possible."

Alyssa did as he bid, never noticing as she descended the staircase and crossed the entry hall that her progress was being watched with considerable interest by the visitor awaiting the duke in the drawing room.

As he joined the duchess there, shutting the door behind him, she demanded, "Whatever in the world is Alyssa doing here?"

Carlyle's jaw dropped in surprise. "You know her?"

"Of course. I am from Northumberland, too," Selena replied in her lilting voice as she seated herself on a sofa upholstered in white brocade. "Why is Alyssa here?"

Contrary to what the world thought, Carlyle and the duchess had never been lovers, but they were close friends of long standing. Nevertheless, he could hardly admit, even to as good a friend as Selena, that he had abducted Alyssa. "More important, why are *you* here?" he asked evasively, settling in an armchair, also covered in white brocade, across from the duchess.

"Curiosity," she replied, her answer as succinct as it was unenlightening. "Now tell me what Alyssa is doing here."

He knew that Selena would not be put off without a plausible answer. If the duchess knew Alyssa when she was living under Lord Eliot's protection in Northumberland, then she had to know, too, what Alyssa was. It surprised His Grace that old Eliot had not kept his incognita's presence at Ormandy Park a secret from the neighborhood. The duke said with a rakish grin, his voice mocking, "Surely you can imagine?"

"If it were any woman except Alyssa I could, but her virtue is above question," the duchess said with such certainty that Carlyle's jaw again dropped in surprise. He had the sudden, uncomfortable feeling that the earth was sinking from beneath his feet.

Selena's eyes suddenly widened in disbelief. "Surely Alyssa cannot be the woman everyone is talking about. I was told the creature's name was Miss Raff."

"What do you know of Miss Raff?"

"The countryside is agog over the report that, for the first time, you have brought one of your ladybirds to Beauchamp. A gorgeous creature named Raff who arrived sans both chaperone and maid, and with only a portmanteau for baggage. That is why I came today. It is so very unlike you that I had to see whether the report was true."

When Carlyle had arrived at Beauchamp with Alyssa, he had done nothing to silence his servants from talking about her presence. Indeed, he had known it would quickly become the talk of the countryside for the very reason that he had never before entertained a woman here. When he had abducted Alyssa, he had been in a rage, intending to make her name so infamous that there would be no danger of her catching another innocent cub like Jeremy in a parson's mousetrap. But now, not only was the evidence mounting that he had been wrong, but his own emotions toward her had altered to the point where he wanted to protect her.

"Alyssa has been nursing my daughter, who has been exceedingly ill." It was not a lie, but neither was it the whole truth. "I truly thought that I would lose Ellen."

To his surprise, the duchess seemed to accept this excuse for Alyssa's presence. "How is the poor child now?"

"Much improved," he said, his relief clearly written on his face. "The fever broke this morning."

"How very fortunate that you were able to secure Alyssa. I doubt that there is a sick person in Northumberland who would not prefer Miss Eliot of Ormandy Park to any doctor. But how on earth did you ever manage to pry her away from her ogre of a grandfather?"

What the devil was Selena talking about? *Miss Eliot of Ormandy Park! Ogre of a grandfather!* Suddenly Carlyle remembered the outrage in Alyssa's eyes that night at the Hagars' when he had exclaimed of Lord Eliot, *"Good God! He is old enough to be your grandfather!"*

"He is—" she had snapped, then stopped. Now at last the duke suspected, to his horror, what the remainder of her sentence would have been.

The duchess, blinking at the dreadful look on her host's face, asked, "Are you ailing, too, Richard? You look in queer stirrups."

"Who is her grandfather?" His voice was suddenly as hoarse as a frog's croak.

The duchess's lovely eyes widened in surprise. "Surely

189

you must know that she is old Lord Eliot's granddaughter.''

His Grace the Duke of Carlyle was once again robbed of speech, a condition that seemed to afflict him with some regularity when the conversation involved Miss Alyssa Raff—or Eliot or whatever the devil her name was.

Selena persisted, ''Surely Alyssa told you that he was her grandfather.''

The duke remembered her insistence after her abduction that Lord Eliot had not been her lover and his own jeering reply: *''Given that magnificent imagination of yours, my dear Miss Raff, what will you try to convince me of next? That the old goat was in reality your grandfather?''* The duke winced as he recalled the despair his answer had brought to her expressive face.

''She tried to,'' he said grimly, ''but I did not believe her.''

''How could you not believe her?'' Selena cried in astonishment. ''Surely one glance assures you of her quality.''

''Yes, it does,'' he admitted grimly, ''but in her case I found it impossible to believe my eyes.''

''I cannot fathom how you managed to get her to Beauchamp without her grandfather's knowing of it.''

Carlyle, although profoundly shaken, managed to mask his dismay beneath a careless demeanor. ''What makes you think that he does not know she is here?''

''Because that old pattern card of propriety would never have permitted her to come to Beauchamp under any circumstances. He is such a high stickler that he will no longer allow me even to see her. My morals do not measure up to Lord Eliot's exacting standards. But compared to you, my dear Richard, I am a paragon of virtue.''

Lord Oldfield's words at Vauxhall echoed in Carlyle's mind: *''The only woman named Alyssa that I know of lives in Northumberland and is as proper a lady of quality as you would ever want to meet."* Why had he not listened more carefully to what that old windbag was saying? Hoarsely, he demanded, "You are certain that she is Lord Eliot's granddaughter?"

The duchess looked at Carlyle as though he had taken leave of his senses. "But, of course, I am. I have known her since she was two years old. That was when her father died, and she came to live with her grandfather. Her papa had been Lord Eliot's heir and favorite son until he allowed himself to be trapped into marrying a vulgar Cit's daughter. By all accounts, she was a truly dreadful woman."

Carlyle, remembering the apparition that had accosted him at Vauxhall, could attest to that.

"After young Eliot's death, she was quite happy to abandon her daughter to her father-in-law to raise, but poor Alyssa was required to spend two weeks with her each summer," Selena continued. "The child used to dread those visits with a passion."

The duke could well imagine that she had. At last, he understood the embarrassed blush that had colored Alyssa's cheeks when he had told her that he had met her mother.

"Not that living with that tyrant, Lord Eliot, was easy." Selena's fingers absently traced the geometrical pattern made by the mahogany-and-rosewood marquetry on a small table beside the sofa. "Try as he might, though, that old curmudgeon never managed to crush Alyssa's spirit. Perhaps that is why she is the only person on earth that he loves. He hardly lets her out of his sight, the selfish old man. He is determined to keep her tied to him until he dies, guarding her from prospective suitors as if she were the crown jewels. The old wretch would not even permit her a London season for fear some young buck would snatch her away from him. He has kept her hidden away, abroad or at Ormandy Park. Despite that, some very eligible young men came courting her, but he drove them all away."

191

The duke suppressed a groan. So much that had baffled him about Alyssa was suddenly clear. The only question he still had was why she had sought to ensnare Jeremy. Or had she? *"It never was a scheme of mine. I could not resist letting you think so after you put me so out of temper at the Hagars', I think understandably so, given your provocation."* Good God, what had he done?

Selena asked abruptly, "Who is Miss Raff?"

"Raff is the name of Alyssa's awful mother. Alyssa has been using it."

"Why?"

"I have no idea. If only I had known her true surname."

"I collect, then, that you truly did not know of Alyssa's connection to Lord Eliot?"

"I knew there was a connection, but I thought that she was his convenient."

"You were mad," the duchess said with strong conviction. "Anyone who knows either Lord Eliot or Alyssa will tell you that." Suddenly she gave Carlyle a sharp, suspicious look. "Alyssa is soft-hearted enough to have been induced to come here to nurse Ellen, but she is much too proper to do so without a chaperone. How *did* you manage to get her here?"

"I abducted her."

"How irregular of you."

"Yes."

"And stupid, too."

"Very stupid," His Grace agreed, "but I was not in possession of all the facts at the time. God, but I could wring her neck. What am I to do with her now?"

The duchess shrugged. "Marry her. Can you do anything else?" Seeing the black look upon his face, she answered her own question. "But yes, of course, *you* can, and knowing your loathing for matrimony, you *will*, too."

"I will not endure a forced marriage of convenience," he ground out through clenched teeth.

192

Selena rose from the sofa. "With all due respect, Alyssa deserved better than you. I must go now. I do not wish to see her. It would only increase her humiliation."

As they reached the door of the library, the duke said, "Swear to me, Selena, that you will say nothing to anyone of Alyssa's presence here."

"Of course I shall say nothing. I like her far too much." She looked at him curiously. "Have you seduced her?"

"No!" he thundered.

"I thought not. But it does not signify. Given your reputation, no one will believe that you have not done so. She is ruined."

Chapter 23

Alyssa waited impatiently on one of the turquoise settees in the library for Carlyle, hoping that at last he would be willing to listen to the truth. She stared out at the gardens, thinking how much she would miss both their beauty and the company of their owner. What would his reaction be when he learned the true relationship between her and Lord Eliot?

The answer to her question came much sooner than she expected. The door to the library was suddenly flung open and Carlyle bounded in, scowling at her as though he meant to serve her head up on a platter.

"Why did you not tell me the truth, Miss Eliot of Ormandy Park?" he demanded fiercely without preamble.

"You would not have believed me," she replied mildly, rising to face him.

"You might have tried me," he said with acerbity. "Why the devil are you not using your own surname?"

She outlined for him the events that led to her living in her mother's house.

"I'll wager your mama did not appreciate your effort on her behalf." Some of the harshness and anger had faded from his voice.

"No," Alyssa said forlornly.

"Why the devil did you bother with her?"

Alyssa looked at him with agonized eyes. "She is my mother. I could not abandon her."

"Why not? She abandoned you when you were in leading strings." Suddenly his scowl disappeared and his golden eyes were disconcertingly sympathetic. "Surely you cannot be happy living with her?"

"No," Alyssa admitted. "I am miserable."

"Why did you not go back to Ormandy Park?"

"Grandpapa would not permit it, at least not yet. You have no notion what a rage he was in when I insisted on going to her. I truly feared that he would have a seizure if I did not agree that I would no longer use his name."

Carlyle began to laugh.

"I fail to see the humor," Alyssa said coldly.

"I was thinking how much more apoplectic that paragon of virtue would be if he learned that you have been passing yourself off as his convenient."

"I did not pass myself off!" she exclaimed. "You assumed! You had your mind made up about what I was before we had even met. I was a scheming strumpet."

He chuckled. "Not to mention a doxy, trollop, vixen, Jezebel, and a few other names that I do not immediately recall." He placed his hands lightly on her arms. "Accept my sincere apologies for my appalling stupidity." His smile and his touch made her heart turn over. "I do think, however, that you owe it to imbeciles such as myself to enlighten them to the errors of their thinking."

She smiled at his self-deprecating humor. How charming he could be. "I am persuaded that even if you had known my true identity, you still would not have wished your son to wed a woman so much older than him."

"You are right on that score, but why would *you* have agreed to marry a stripling? It was not, I have now learned, because you lacked for eligible suitors."

"It was never my intention to marry him. I had no desire for such a mésalliance. The difference in our ages was even

195

more unacceptable to me than to you, and I did not love him.''

His hands dropped from her arms, and his face darkened into a scowl. ''What the devil, then, was your intention in accepting his offer—to break his heart?''

''Just the opposite. To spare both his heart and his pride. You, as much as anyone, must understand how sensitive and easily wounded both are when a calfling is in the throes of his first infatuation. I did not actually accept his offer. I only agreed not to reject it. He is so very stubborn that I knew to do so would only make him all the more mulishly determined to win me.''

As Alyssa talked, Carlyle's expression lightened. ''What a masterful understanding you have of my son,'' he said admiringly.

His compliment thrilled her, and she flashed him a grateful smile. ''You did not believe me, but I do care very much about Jeremy. My affection, however, is that of a sister for a younger brother. I could not bear to trample on either his heart or his pride. I thought it would be so much less painful for him if only he could come to see for himself that I was not the woman for him. I let him think that I would accept his offer while I strove to demonstrate to him that we would not suit. I swore him to secrecy about the betrothal to provide him time to make that discovery. I knew it would not take me long to give him a disgust of me.''

An odd light shone in the duke's eyes. ''I profess an enormous curiosity as to how you thought you could manage to do that.''

''I treated him as an overbearing, criticizing matriarch would treat a grandson still in leading strings,'' she replied candidly.

His lips twitched. ''Were you truly successful in curing his tendre for you?''

"Of course. I was so odious that I could hardly stand myself."

He laughed softly. "So you were telling me the truth about his crying off the betrothal?"

His laugh warmed her, and she smiled rather shyly at him. "Yes, I told you that the story would have a happy ending for all of us." But it would not end happily for her. Not now that she had fallen hopelessly in love with Carlyle.

"Which means you were also telling me the truth about the real purpose of your journey to Gretna Green. Why the devil did Jeremy not tell me what he was up to?"

"He was certain that you would put a stop to it. He said that you abhorred elopements so much that no circumstances, no matter how dire, would make one acceptable to you."

"It is true I did tell him that, but only because I was trying to dissuade him from making for the border with you," Carlyle confessed. "In truth, I approve of Sarah Turner's eloping with George Braden. Stokes would be the death of her. I must say, however, that I never thought that George would have the gumption to do it."

"He hadn't. Nor the money, either. That was where Jeremy came in. He provided both."

"Good for Jeremy," Carlyle said with a smile that suddenly faded as he regarded Alyssa. "Why the devil didn't you confide to me what you were about that first night at the Hagars'?"

"I started to, but you cut me off and began calling me all those dreadful names. No one had ever questioned either my character or my virtue before, and I was so outraged I could not resist letting you think the worst."

"That was stupid of you."

"Yes, I know that now," she admitted, "but at the time I had no notion that you would abduct me."

"Now that I have," he asked grimly, "what do you want from me?"

She blinked in surprise at his question. "Your apology. And to be returned to London as quickly as possible."

"What?" He stared at her incredulously.

Why should he look so thunderstruck? Alyssa wondered. It was not so very much that she was asking. "Surely, Your Grace, you owe me that much!"

"I owe you a good deal more," he said dryly. "Your stay here without chaperone or maid is the talk of the countryside. The world believes you to be my mistress."

"But so long as it thinks me to be Miss Raff, it does not signify."

He regarded her with amazement. "I must congratulate you on how calmly you are taking your ruin."

"I do not believe that I am ruined yet, although I shall not rest easy on that score until I am back in London. My liveliest fear is that my mama will find out that I am here. She would immediately go to my grandfather." Alyssa's voice faltered, and she clenched her hands tightly together. "I could not bear for him to know."

"Why would she go to him?" Carlyle asked, his voice as gentle as a summer breeze.

"She would not tell me what you said to her at Vauxhall, but whatever it was, she hates you even more than she hates my grandfather. She would like nothing so much as to make enormous trouble for you, and she knows Grandpapa would do so."

"Would you not like to do so as well, after all that I have said and done to you?" he asked, a curious light in his eyes.

"Of course not. Why should I?"

"I can think of a number of good reasons," he said softly, regarding her in the oddest way.

She shrugged. "I have no one to blame but myself for not having been honest with you in the beginning. Now

198

that I have seen how much you love your children and have heard the unhappy story of your marriage, I understand why you were so determined to protect Jeremy from similar misery.''

"Who told you about my marriage?" he demanded sharply.

"Lady Hester." Her answer, however, was drowned out by a loud disturbance in the hall.

"What the devil now?" Carlyle demanded.

An instant later the door of the library was flung open and Jeremy rushed in.

Chapter 24

Carlyle paled at the sight of his note in Jeremy's hand.

"Papa, I was *not*—" Jeremy broke off as he saw Alyssa. "So you did come here! I can scarcely believe it. How could you tell my father such lies?"

The duke flinched. "Jeremy, she did not—"

But his son interrupted, crying passionately, "I was not running away with her! I was only helping Sarah Turner and George Braden to elope. Alyssa and I were no longer even betrothed! How glad I am now that I had cried off!" His voice quavered with outrage and scorn as he faced her. "I have never been so excessively shocked in my life as I am by your treacherous behavior. To dare to tell my father that we were eloping, after I had broken off our engagement. Was that why you were so understanding about it? You were planning to use me to extort a carte blanche from him. You are brazen beyond belief! You are not at all the woman I thought you to be!"

Alyssa saw the bleakness and despair in Carlyle's eyes as he started to speak. He meant to tell Jeremy the truth, knowing that the rage now being directed at her would be turned on him. The trusting relationship that he had so carefully built with his son over the years would be irrevocably ruptured. A huge lump swelled in her throat, and she knew that she could not let this happen.

The duke began sadly, "Jeremy, you—"

Alyssa hastily interrupted him, saying icily to Jeremy, "Of course I am not the woman you thought me to be. You had already learned that, had you not? That is why you cried off our betrothal. Why, then, should you be so shocked now?"

Jeremy stared at her in such disgust that she wanted to cry. It broke her heart to have him despise her like this, but better her than his father.

"I hate you, you wicked woman!" he cried, and would have run from the room.

But the doorway was blocked by Mrs. Raff who, having been defeated by her huge skirt in her attempt to enter the room in the usual manner, was now sidling into it sideways, looking rather like an inverted purple mushroom.

"Good God," Carlyle exclaimed in profound shock at the sight of the grapes, strawberries, apricots, and tamarinds piled high on Mrs. Raff's hat, "it is a walking orchard."

Alyssa groaned in despair at the sight of her mother. To her surprise, the duke reached out and gave her arm a comforting squeeze before turning back to face the latest intruder. Mrs. Raff at last managed to clear the doorway, permitting Jeremy to escape, and he slammed the door so hard that Alyssa winced.

Mrs. Raff immediately launched her offensive. "You may fob that silly boy off with nonsense about seeking a carte blanche, Alyssa, but I know you better. You are such a pattern of propriety that you would never, never consider such a thing."

"You are quite right, madam," the duke interjected coolly. "It was I who made the offer to her."

Although clearly startled by this admission, Mrs. Raff hastened to take advantage of it. "And when she refused you, you abducted her. But now you will pay the price. Even a duke cannot go about kidnapping innocent ladies of quality and ruining them without paying the piper! I shall see that all England knows of your abduction of my daughter." She smirked at him triumphantly. "It *will* be the scandal of the *millennium*."

"Mama, no," Alyssa cried, determined to stop her mother. "It is I who ruined myself. I . . . I"—she closed her eyes for an instant, gathering her courage to utter the lie that was forming on her lips—"I accepted his carte blanche."

"I do not believe it!" Mrs. Raff snapped.

"But I did," Alyssa replied calmly, "so there is no use in your creating a scandal, for it is we who shall be embarrassed, not him."

"You sapskull!" her mother screeched. "How could you settle for that when you could have had so much more?"

"What more? A loveless marriage to a man who was forced to wed me?" Out of the corner of her eye, Alyssa saw that Carlyle was watching her intently as she spoke. "I prefer a carte blanche, and you can do nothing about it, Mama."

"Oh, but I can! You will not be so brass-faced when your grandfather comes."

Alyssa visibly blanched. "Please do not involve Grandpapa in this."

"I most certainly shall. He will be notified of your scandalous behavior by the next mail." She smirked. "I am confident that he will be here posthaste when he learns what you have agreed to."

"You need not trouble Lord Eliot with word of that, for I have withdrawn my offer to your daughter of a carte blanche," Carlyle said languidly. "Nothing on earth could induce me to grant her one now."

Mrs. Raff was much taken aback that not only did the duke know the identity of Alyssa's illustrious grandfather, but was not at all concerned by it. However, she was not a woman who gave up easily. "First you make her false

202

promises, then you abduct her, ruin her, and now you cast her upon the world with nothing at all.'' Her shrill voice trembled with righteous indignation. ''Well, you will not succeed! Neither I nor her grandfather—and you will find that he is a man of considerable influence—will settle for anything less than your doing right by her.''

''Save your breath, madam,'' Carlyle said coldly. ''It is my intention to do so.''

For a moment, Mrs. Raff was speechless, looking like a sail that had suddenly lost the wind. ''Is it?'' she scoffed at last. ''Let me tell you that there is only one way that you can do that! You must marry her!''

''But of course,'' Carlyle said as casually as though he were agreeing to tea with breakfast.

Both mother and daughter gaped at him in openmouthed astonishment.

Mrs. Raff was the first to recover. The look of malicious triumph that gleamed on her mama's face tore at Alyssa. Mrs. Raff pressed her victory, insisting, ''You must wed her at once.''

''The sooner the better,'' His Grace agreed amicably.

''You are mad!'' Alyssa cried.

''Probably,'' he replied carelessly.

''You cannot marry me!''

''I can and I shall.''

''No, you shall not!'' Alyssa cried frantically. ''I refuse to marry you.''

''You stupid fool!'' screamed Mrs. Raff, so vexed that she reached out to box her daughter's ears, only to find her wrist captured in the duke's punishing grip.

''Do not dare!'' he snapped. ''There is, madam, one condition to my agreeing to marry your daughter. It is that you are not welcome in my house *now* or *ever*. Take it or leave it.''

Mrs. Raff reverted to outraged mother. ''You think that

I would leave my innocent daughter unprotected under your roof until you are wed?"

"Why not?" he asked coldly. "You deserted her when she was in leading strings and needed you more. Furthermore, you cannot argue her innocence needs protecting in one breath, and in the next that I must marry her because I have robbed her of it."

Mrs. Raff tossed her head so indignantly that the fruit wobbled precariously atop her hat.

The duke said blandly, "I would not shake the tree too hard, madam. You run the risk of losing your fruit—and a ducal son-in-law." His hard, glittering eyes bored into her, and a cynical smile played about his lips. "Of course, the world need not know that he refuses to receive you unless you choose to tell it."

A bitter half smile quirked Alyssa's mouth at how well Carlyle understood the workings of her mother's mind.

Mrs. Raff contemplated his veiled ultimatum, then turned abruptly and walked to the door, where her exit was promptly halted by the width of her skirt. She uttered a strangled expletive that should never sully a lady's lips, viciously crushed her skirt to her, and ramroded it through the doorway into the hall.

The duke followed her to the door, beckoning to Pedley who was standing just beyond it. "See that she is returned to London immediately." His Grace smiled urbanely at his longtime retainer, whose ears were as sharp as a hunting hound's. "It comforts me, Pedley, to know how deaf you are. It would be a great pity should anything that transpired in this room be repeated outside of it to anyone—anyone at all."

Master and servant exchanged looks of perfect understanding.

"Furthermore, Miss *Raff* has departed with her mama. Neither you nor any of the other servants have yet seen Miss *Eliot*, who is about to become my wife."

Another look was exchanged between the two men before the duke shut the door and strode back to Alyssa.

"That will not stop the talk," she said.

He smiled sardonically. "Will it not? My servants are very well paid, and I am considered an excellent master."

"Let me go back to London, too. I do not want to marry you."

"I know you do not," he said grimly, "but I promise you that it need be nothing more than a marriage of convenience." His distaste for his proposal was very clear in the harsh lines of his face. "We can go our separate ways. You need see me only rarely, and I will not demand intimacy."

These assurances were clearly meant to quiet Alyssa's objections, but they only strengthened them, filling her with profound despair. She could imagine no more exquisitely painful form of torture than a marriage in name only to this man whom she loved. And how he must hate the prospect of being trapped in a dreadful mésalliance that he wanted even less for himself than he had for his son. Once again, he would be bound to a woman whom he did not love. Remembering the loathing on his face when he had glanced at his late wife's portrait, Alyssa's heart shattered at the thought of him looking at her like that.

Misinterpreting her agonized look, he continued to try to soothe her doubts. "You will have more freedom than you do now. I promise to ask very little of you."

"What *will* you ask of me, Your Grace?"

There was a fleeting look of ineffable sadness in his eyes. "Only that you accept my name. I cannot, under the circumstances, insist upon fidelity, but I ask that you be discreet and do not embarrass me. I shall do the same for you."

His words froze Alyssa to the marrow. How utterly miserable she would be, knowing that the husband she loved was with other women. She cried in revulsion, "Surely you cannot want such a marriage, either!"

"Of course I do not want it!" he snapped impatiently. "But I have no choice."

"I do, and I choose not to marry you!"

"You have none, either," he said irritably. "Don't be a paperskull, Alyssa. Your vulgar mother will create a scandal that will put you beyond the pale of polite society if you do not marry me."

"I do not care!" she cried, her dimpled chin rising to a defiant angle.

"Well, I do." There was a glint of amusement in his gold-flecked eyes. "My honor as well as yours is at stake."

His flash of humor disconcerted her. "You are already notorious," she protested.

"I may be notorious, but I am not yet infamous, and I have no desire to become so."

"You are quizzing me."

"No," he said quietly. "My morals are not quite as black as you think. I abide by the rules of the game. Your vulgar mama is correct. One does not abduct and ruin virtuous ladies of quality, then cast them off."

"You have not ruined me!"

"But when your loving mama is done, the world will think I have. And that is the same thing. What will you do then? Your grandfather will not take you back. Nor will your mama, if you deny her a duke for a son-in-law, even one who will not permit her in his house."

"I will find a position as a governess or a teacher in a young ladies' seminary," she said with quiet determination. The thought of what a dreary life she would lead filled her with dread, but not nearly as much dread as being married to a man she adored, when he did not return her love.

"I cannot think that either career would be of long duration once your mother has brewed her scandal broth," he said softly.

He was right, of course, and Alyssa could not keep the dismay from her face.

Seeing it, he said quietly, "We shall be married by special license tomorrow."

Alyssa felt as if she were suffocating. "I beg of you to give me a little time to adjust to the idea," she pleaded, determined to escape before the deed was done.

As if reading her mind, he said with amusement, "It is not time to adjust that you want, but time to flee."

Seeing the spots of color rise in her cheeks, he laughed. "Don't try to run. You will succeed only in making me very angry."

"You would be well rid of me if I did flee," she replied candidly.

"I will be the judge of that," he said, smiling. "Only recollect there is my reputation to be saved. Now promise that you will marry me on the morrow."

"No, I cannot!" she cried defiantly.

"Why not?" he demanded, his good humor giving way to irritation.

"I cannot, for it would be a lie. And I will not lie to you."

"That is *some* consolation," he said dryly. "Why do you fight me like this when I am only trying to do what is honorable?"

"I wish that you had not discovered honor at this late date!"

His eyes narrowed speculatively. "Is it my reputation that makes you so determined not to marry me?"

She looked away, no longer able to meet his penetrating eyes, and stammered, "You are reputed to love the ladies—a great many of them."

"No, I loved none of them."

"You said you loved your wife."

"At first. I was barely sixteen and green as grass when I was married to a woman years older and decades more sophisticated than I, a woman I hardly knew and who easily dazzled such a rustic calfling as I was.'' He gave a harsh, contemptuous laugh at the memory that tore at Alyssa's heart. ''I had never had a woman; I had never even been to London. I was such a flat that I thought all marriages were like my parents'—they adored each other. I had a quick and brutal education. My wife lacked the concern for a stripling's heart and pride that you exhibited toward Jeremy. It gave her considerable pleasure to trample on both.''

Alyssa stood very still, her fingernails unconsciously digging into her palms, her heart breaking. The naked pain in his eyes all these years later told her how cruelly his wife had wounded him. It was all that Alyssa could do to keep from putting her arms around him and comforting him. No wonder he had been so enraged when he had thought that history was repeating itself with Jeremy.

Carlyle's face twisted cynically. ''In time I discovered that, unlike my wife, a great many women were not only delighted to have my attention but actively pursued my, er, companionship. I did not fool myself that my charm was what attracted them as much as my title and fortune. But after my disastrous marriage, I found it amusing to be courted rather than rejected.''

The self-mockery in his voice hurt Alyssa almost as much as his pain had a moment earlier. No wonder he had so little affection for members of her sex.

''I was not averse to indulging in brief affairs.'' Wry amusement flickered in his hazel eyes. ''Not nearly as many, however, as is rumored, or I would be dead of exhaustion. Not a very honorable story, I grant you, but I never before abducted a woman, virtuous or otherwise, and ruined her. I will not do so now.''

She tried another argument. ''You cannot marry me, Your Grace. Only think how Jeremy hates me.''

''Yes.'' Carlyle studied her curiously for a moment.

"Why did you try to protect me instead of telling him the truth?"

"It was better that he hate me instead of you," she said sadly. "I could not stand to be the cause of an estrangement between you. You were only attempting to save him from a dreadful mistake."

He smiled sadly, touching the dimple in her chin lightly with the tip of his finger. "I know that you meant well, and I am grateful. But he must know the truth."

"Oh, what a mull I have made of things!" Alyssa cried, her shoulders slumping in dejection.

He reached up and stroked Alyssa's cheek lightly, comfortingly, with his long, graceful fingers. "I have given you my word that ours need be a marriage in name only. Now give me your word that you will accept it."

His touch thrilled her so that it was difficult to deny him anything. But his confession about his marriage only made her all the more determined that she would not be responsible for his being married again to a woman that he did not want. "No," she reiterated, staring miserably down at floor.

"Why must you be so difficult?" he demanded in exasperation. His fingers moved to her chin, tipping it up. He glared darkly into her eyes. "I am not a patient man. I am attempting to do what is right; but good intentions, when they run contrary to what I want, do not come easily to me. And I do not want this marriage of convenience, so do not test your luck."

His final sentence filled her simultaneously with despair and hope. He did not want to marry her. If she fled him, he might make no effort to reclaim her.

Carlyle's hands moved to her cheeks, holding her face gently so that she had to meet his curious eyes. "Is marrying me such a terrible fate?" he asked softly.

His touch and his unexpected tenderness undermined Alyssa's self-control. Try as she might, she could not keep the tears from her eyes. Wedding him would be heaven if only he loved her and wanted a true marriage, not a charade whose only purpose was to spare her reputation. "Yes," she choked.

He stared sadly into her teary eyes for a long moment, then said, "I know that I have given you no reason to like me, Alyssa."

"Nor I you, Your Grace," she replied shakily, trying to blink back her tears. "If only I had not let my anger rule my head that night at the Hagars'."

"Yes, if only," he said, his tone suddenly savage, "but you did, and now I fear I must pay a dreadful price!"

As she blinked in surprise at his sudden, inexplicable anger, he turned and stalked from the room.

Tears flowed unchecked down her cheeks as his final words echoed and reechoed in her mind: *"And now I fear I must pay a dreadful price!"*

No! Alyssa would not let him. She clenched her hands into determined little balls. "I will escape you somehow."

Chapter 25

Minutes later, a messenger was dispatched on the fleetest horse in Beauchamp's stables with Carlyle's hastily scrawled instructions to Hugh Page for a special license.

Then His Grace, learning that Jeremy was with his sister, hurried up the broad marble staircase, determined to get his unhappy confession to his son over with at once. The door to Ellen's room was open, and his children's voices drifted out.

"Papa brought the most lovely lady to nurse me," Ellen said. "I think I should like her for a mama. Her name is Alyssa."

"You are touched in the upperworks," Jeremy growled. "She is the most dreadful woman I have ever met."

Ellen gasped in protest. "She is not!"

"Of course she is not," Carlyle said, entering the room and striding rapidly to his daughter's bedside. "How are you feeling, my pet?"

"Much better, Papa."

And he saw that she was. The fever was gone, and her brown eyes were once again bright and clear. He bent to kiss her. "I am so pleased, my pet." Turning to his son, he said, "Come, Jeremy, I must talk to you."

The boy followed his father into the private sitting room that was part of the ducal apartments. It was a cheerful spot with informal portraits of Carlyle's children, parents, brothers, and sisters at various ages lining its walls.

The duke led his son to a pair of beechwood chairs by a window that overlooked the gardens. When they were both seated, he asked Jeremy, "Why did you not tell me the truth about the trip you were planning to Gretna Green?"

"You would have forbidden me to aid in an elopement."

"To the contrary, in George and Sarah's case, I would have helped you. As it was, I knew you were lying to me, but not why. I erroneously concluded that it was you who was eloping with Alyssa."

"But we were no longer even betrothed."

"I could hardly have suspected that, when you asked me for eight hundred pounds to buy her a betrothal gift," Carlyle noted dryly.

Jeremy hung his head. "I hated lying to you, Papa. It is the first time I have ever done so."

"Deceit breeds deceit, my dear boy. I was so outraged by what I thought was happening that I, in turn, lied to you in my note about Alyssa coming to me. She did not."

"Then why is she here?" Jeremy asked in confusion.

"I was determined to prevent her from eloping with you because I knew you would not suit. So I abducted her."

Jeremy gasped. "You cannot mean her dreadful mama was right?"

"Unfortunately, yes."

"But Alyssa said—"

"She said only that she was not the woman you thought her to be. She was attempting to deflect your anger from me because she blames herself for the misunderstanding that led to my abducting her."

Jeremy groaned. "Her mama will make a dreadful scandal!"

"No."

212

"How will you prevent it?"

"The only way I can. By marrying Alyssa."

"Oh, no, Papa, you cannot," Jeremy cried in horrified accents. "She is a termagant!"

Carlyle's lips twitched as he remembered Alyssa's words: *"I was so odious that I could hardly stand myself."*

"A gentleman does not abduct ladies of quality and not marry them."

Jeremy shuddered. "You can have no notion how overbearing and managing she can be."

"I have a good notion," the duke said in amusement. "Do you think I will not be master in my own house? Surely you know *me* better than that, Jeremy."

His son's face lightened. "Of course *you* will know how to handle her."

Carlyle did not share his son's conviction. Nothing in his broad experience with women had prepared him for Miss Alyssa Eliot, and he was far from certain how to achieve his objective with her.

Alyssa remained in her room, refusing to go downstairs for dinner because she was embarrassed at how red her eyes were from weeping over the cruel twist of fate that would make the man she loved her husband in name only. Nor did she want to face him or his son.

Before retiring for the night, however, she went to Ellen's room to check on her a final time and found Carlyle bending over his daughter, bidding her a tender good night. As Alyssa watched them, a horrifying question assailed her: Was Ellen his daughter? Just then he rose and turned toward the door, seeing Alyssa's question reflected in her eyes. His eyes narrowed angrily, but he said nothing, only nodded at her and left the room abruptly.

Surely, he could not know what she was thinking, Alyssa told herself as she went to Ellen's side, where she was heartened to see how much normal color had returned to the girl's cheeks.

"How are you feeling?" Alyssa asked gently as she felt the invalid's forehead and soothed back her tangled brown curls.

"Much better," Ellen said, staring up at her visitor with frank curiosity. "Papa says you are going to become my mama. I think I shall like that."

"Would you?" Alyssa asked as she squeezed the girl's thin hand.

"Yes, I think so. Jeremy does not like it very much, though. He says you are very bossy and shrewish, but Papa says that I am not to worry. You will not be like that." The girl's brown eyes, suddenly worried, searched Alyssa's. "Will you mind that I am an invalid, or do you think you can love me?"

"I would love you very much," Alyssa cried, her voice catching. She bent down and kissed Ellen's cool forehead. "Good night, little one."

When Alyssa emerged into the hall, Carlyle was waiting there for her. "To answer your silent question," he said coldly, "Ellen is my daughter in every respect, save perhaps biologically."

He *was* a mind reader! Alyssa thought, mortified that he had guessed what she was thinking.

"Even biologically, it is possible, indeed probable, that I am her father."

Alyssa remembered what Hester had said about the month that he had spent closeted with his wife in London before they went their separate ways.

"But it matters not," he continued. "Make no mistake: to me, Ellen is my child. I would never want her to have the tiniest doubt of it."

Alyssa looked at him with glowing eyes. "How good you are!"

As he looked into her expressive face, his breath caught,

and he held it for an instant before saying briskly, "Nonsense! Innocent children should not be made to pay for their parents' failings."

He took Alyssa's arm and pulled her hastily into his private sitting room lined with informal portraits of his family. She started to protest, but he silenced her saying, "I only want to talk. Your honor is safe with me."

"Too safe," she answered tartly.

"What do you mean by that?"

"We would both be happier if you forgot both it and marrying me."

His penetrating eyes were studying her face. "How red your eyes are." His thick brows knit together in a scowl. "You said to me earlier that you would not lie to me. Tell me the truth, now. Is the thought of marrying me so utterly reprehensible to you?"

"No," she admitted miserably, staring at the wall beyond his head.

"Then why are you being so damned stubborn?" he exploded.

Tears glistened in her eyes. "I am trying to save you from a marriage of convenience that you do not want."

His thick brows raised like twin question marks. "Trying to save *me*, my dear Alyssa?" He stared at her for a long, startled moment before continuing cheerfully, "Well, and so you have. I withdraw my offer of such a marriage." He grinned so happily at her that her heart seemed to split in two. "I warned you not to push your luck too far."

"Thank God," she murmured, trying to sound delighted, but it was exceedingly difficult to do so because the giant lump that had formed in her throat at his words was choking her. Now that she had achieved her goal, all she wanted was to throw herself on her bed and sob her heart out. Struggling to retain her composure, she bowed her head and said quietly, "I will leave in the morning."

"Much as it pains me to deny you anything, my dear Alyssa, that is not possible," he replied firmly. "I shall require your company at Beauchamp for a considerable time yet."

"But . . . but you just said that you were withdrawing your offer of marriage."

"Yes, I am rescinding my offer of a marriage of convenience. Now I intend to have the kind of union with you that I want."

"A carte blanche?" she gasped, whitening.

"Good God, no! I want that no more than I want a pallid charade. I wish ours to be a real marriage in every sense of the word."

"But you neither love nor want me."

His gold-flecked eyes regarded her in astonishment. "Peagoose! But of course I love you! Why the devil else would I want you to be my life's companion?"

Her eyes widened in startled disbelief. He laughed and drew her into his arms. Slowly, lovingly, his sensual mouth descended on hers, and he kissed her with a fierce passion that demanded and received a like response from her. When at last he lifted his head, her heart was beating in triple time, her arms remained tightly around him, and she radiated a happiness that was reflected back at her from his gold-flecked eyes.

She stared at him wonderingly. "But if you love me, why did you offer me a marriage of convenience?"

He stroked her hair tenderly. "I was certain that after all that I had done and said to you, you would reject anything more. I hoped that after we were married I could in time make you care for me—although I was far from certain of that. I was so afraid that I would be condemned to a sham of a marriage with you, when I wanted so much more." He hugged her as though he feared that she might somehow still escape him. "Why did you refuse my proposal? I was trying to be understanding."

"What was so understanding about telling me that I was free to take other lovers, when I want none ever but you?" she demanded indignantly.

He laughed, a deep, happy, possessive laugh. "You might have enlightened me."

"I did not think that you wanted either me or my love."

"Not want you, you divine creature? My God, I was jealous of my own son. And furious at your grandfather, too. If I had met him before I learned the truth about your relationship, I doubt that he would have survived the encounter! I have been fascinated by you since that day we met in the park."

"So fascinated that you did not even ask my name!"

He chuckled, and his finger traced her lips lightly. "I knew that would pique you. When I did find out who you were, I was utterly baffled by the contradiction between what you seemed and what you were." He sighed unhappily. "If only I had listened to my instincts."

"Instead, you were determined to think the worst of me."

"With a good deal of assistance from you and that vulgar mama of yours," he retorted with a grin.

The glow faded from Alyssa's face at the mention of her mother, and she felt it her unhappy duty to try once again to bring Carlyle to his senses. "Only think what a dreadful mésalliance you will be making if you marry me."

"Not a mésalliance, my darling, a grand alliance!"

She could not help giggling, but still she persisted. "Recollect that you swore you would move heaven and earth to keep me from being the next duchess of Carlyle."

"Now I would happily move both to assure that you are. Moving them, however, is not half so formidable a task as winning your consent, my stubborn lady of the laburnum."

Her eyes glowed mischievously. "But remember how easily you bore."

He sighed. "I see that you mean to throw every foolish

thing that I said to you back in my teeth. Boredom is the least of my fears with you. I may come to yearn for it occasionally." His mouth poised above hers, so close that his warm breath caressed her lips. "Are you going to marry me tomorrow?"

She smiled, eyes brimming with her love for him. "If you insist."

His lips brushed hers lightly, tantalizingly. "I most emphatically insist."

"But you never again wanted anything to do with matrimony, Your Grace."

He grinned. "And you proved me wrong, as you have so often since we met. Now stop calling me Your Grace; my name is Richard."

Her face glowed impishly. "Much as it pains me to deny you anything," she said, deliberately echoing his earlier words to her, "I prefer 'my love.' "